Ebony& Crystal

Poems

In

Verse

And

Prose

Pocket Edition

Clark Ashton Smith

Ebony and Crystal
Clark Ashton Smith
Pocket Edition
2023
ISBN: 978-0-6457432-0-3

This pocket edition made available by Jonathon Best.

View more pocket editions and other books at
Jbestbooks.com

Contents

PREFACE

Who of us care to be present at the accouchment of the immortal? I think that we so attend who are first to take this book in our hands. A bold assertion, truly, and one demonstrable only in years remote from these; and—dust wages no war with dust. But it is one of those things that I should most "like to come back and see."

Because he has lent himself the more innocently to the whispers of his subconscious daemon, and because he has set those murmurs to purer and harder crystal than we others, by so much the longer will the poems of Clark Ashton Smith endure. Here indeed is loot against the forays of moth and rust. Here we shall find none or little of the sentimental fat with which so much of our literature is larded. Rather shall one in

Imagination's "misty mid-region," see elfin rubies burn at his feet, witch-fires glow in the nearer cypresses, and feel upon his brow a wind from the unknown. The brave hunters of fly-specks on Art's cathedral windows will find little here for their trouble, and both the stupid and the over-sophisticated would best stare owlishly and pass by: here are neither kindergartens nor skyscrapers. But let him who is worthy by reason of his clear eye and unjaded heart wander across these borders of beauty and mystery and be glad.

GEORGE STERLING.
San Francisco, October 28, 1922.

Arabesque

Like arabesques of ebony,
The cypresses, in silhouette,
Fantastically cleave and fret
A moon of yellow ivory.

The coldly colored rays illume
A leafy pattern manifold,
And all the field is overscrolled
With curiously figured gloom.

Like arabesques of ebony,
Or like Arabian lattices,
Forever seem the cypresses
Before a moon of ivory.

Beyond the Great Wall

Beyond the far Cathayan wall,
A thousand leagues athwart the sky,
The scarlet stars and mornings die,
The gilded moons and sunsets fall.

Across the sulphur-colored sands
With bales of silk the camels fare,
Harnessed with vermil and with vair,
Into the blue and burning lands.

And, ah, the song the drivers sing,
To while the desert leagues away—
A song they sang in old Cathay,
Ere youth had left the eldest king,—

Ere love and beauty both grew old,
And wonder and romance were flown
On fiery wings to worlds unknown,
To stars of undiscovered gold.

And I their alien words would know,
And follow past the lonely Wall,
Where gilded moons and sunsets fall,
As in a song of long ago.

To Omar Khayyam

Omar, within thy scented garden-close,
When passed with eventide
The starward incense of the waning rose—
Too fair and dear and precious to abide
After the glad and golden death of spring—
Omar, thou heardest then,
Above the world of men,
The mournful rumour of an iron wing,
The sough and sigh of desolating years,
Whereof the wind is as the winds that blow
Out of a lonesome land of night and snow,
Where ancient winter weeps with frozen tears;
And in thy bodeful ears,
The brief and tiny lisp
Of petals curled and crisp,
Fallen at Eve in Persia's mellow clime,
Was mingled with the mighty sound of time.
Omar, thou knewest well
How the fair days are sorrowful and strange
With time's inexorable mystery
And terror ineluctable of change:
Upon thine eyes the bleak and bitter spell
Of vision, thou didst see,
As in a magic glass,
The moulded mists and painted shadows pass—
The ghostly pomps we name reality.
And, lo, the level field,
With broken fane and throne,
And dust of old, unfabled cities sown,
In unremembering years was made to yield,

From out the shards of Pow'r,
The pillars frail and small
That lift for capital
The blood-like bubble of the poppy-flow'r;
And crowns were crumbled for the airy gold
The crocus and the daffodil should hold
As inalienable dow'r.
Before thy gaze, the sad unvaried green
The cypresses like robes funereal wear,
Was woven on the gradual looms of air,
From threadbare silk and tattered sendaline
That clothed some ancient queen;
And from the spoilt vermilion of her mouth,
The myrtles rose, and from her ruined hair,
And eyes that held the summer's ardent drouth
In blown, forgotten bow'rs;
And amber limbs and breast,
Through ancient nights by sleepless love

                                   oppressed,

Or by the iron flight of loveless hours.
Knowing the weary wisdom of the years,
The empty truth of tears;
The suns of June, that with some great excess
Of ardour slay the unabiding rose,
And grey-haired winter, wan and fervourless
For whom no flower grows;
Seeing the scarlet and the gold that pales,
On Orient snows untrod,
In magic morns that grant,
Across a land of common green and gray,
The disenchanted day;
Knowing the iron veils
And walls of adamant,

That ward the flaming verities of God—
Knowing these things, ah, surely thou wert wise,
Beneath the warm and thunder-dreaming skies,
To kiss on ardent breast and avid mouth,
Some girl whose sultry eyes
Were golden with the sun-beloved south—
To pluck the rose and drain the rose-red wine,
In gardens half-divine;
Before the broken cup
Be filled and covered up
In dusty seas of everlasting drouth.

Rosa Mystica

The secret rose we vainly dream to find,
Was blown in grey Atlantis long ago,
Or in old summers of the realms of snow,
Its attar lulled the pole-arisen wind;
Or once its broad and breathless petals pined
In gardens of Persepolis, aglow
With desert sunlight, and the fiery, slow
Red waves of sand, invincible and blind.

On orient isles, or isles hesperian,
Through mythic days ere mortal time began,
It flowered above the ever-flowering foam;
Or, legendless, in lands of yesteryear,
It flamed among the violets—near, how near,
To unenchanted fields and hills of home!

Strangeness

O love, thy lips are bright and cold,
Like jewels carven curiously
To symbols of a mystery,
A secret dim, forgotten, old.

Like woven amber, finely spun,
Thy hair, enwoofed with golden light,
Remembers yet the flaming flight
Of some unknown, archaic sun.

Thine eyes are crystals green and chill,
Wherein, as in a shifting sea,
Wan fires and drowning splendours flee
To stealthy deeps forever still.

Fallen across thy dreaming face,
The dawn is made a secret thing,
Like flame of crimson lamps that swing
At midnight, in a cavern-space.

Thy smile is like the furtive gleam
Of fleeing moons a traveller sees
Through closing arms of cypress-trees,
In secret realms of night and dream.

Sphinx-like, unsolved eternally,
Thy beauty's riddle doth abide,
And love hath come, and love hath died,
Striving to read the mystery.

The Nereid

Her face the sinking stars desire.
Unto her place the slow deeps bring
Shadow of errant winds that wing
O'er sterile gulfs of foam and fire.

Her beauty is the light of pearls.
All stars and dreams and sunsets die
To make the fluctuant glooms that lie
Around her, and low noonlight swirls

Down ocean's firmamental deep,
To weave for her who glimmers there,
Elusive visions, vague and fair;
And night is as a dreamless sleep:

She has not known the night's unrest,
Nor the white curse of clearer day;
The tremors of the tempest play
Like slow delight about her breast.

Serene, an immanence of fire,
She dwells forever, ocean-thralled,
Soul of the sea's vast emerald;
Her face the sinking stars desire.

In Saturn

Upon the seas of Saturn I have sailed
To isles of high, primeval amarant,
Where the flame-tongued sonorous flow'rs
                              enchant
The hanging surf to silence: All engrailed

With ruby-colored pearls, the golden shore
Allured me; but as one whom spells restrain,
For blind horizons of the sombre main,
And harbors never known, my singing prore

I set forthrightly: Formed of fire and brass,
Immenser skies divided, deep on deep
Before me,—till, above the darkling foam,
With dome on cloudless adamantine dome,
Black peaks no peering seraph deems to pass,
Rose up from realms ineffable as Sleep!

Impression

The silver silence of the moon
Upon the sleeping garden lies;
The wind of evening dies,
As in forgetful dreams a ghostly tune.

How white, how still, the flowers are,
As carved of pearl and ivory!
The pines are ebony,
A sombre frieze on heavens pale and far.

Like mirrors made of lucid stone,
The pools lie calm, and bright, and cold,
Where moon and stars behold,
In some eternal trance, themselves alone.

Triple Aspect

Lo, for Earth's manifest monotony
Of ordered aspect unto sun and star,
And single moon, I turn to years afar,
And ampler worlds ensphered in memory.

There, to the zoned and iris-differing light
Of three swift suns in heavens of vaster range,
Transcendant Beauty knows a trinal change,
And dawn and eve are in the place of night.

There, long ago, in mornings ocean-green,
I saw bright deserts dusky with the sky,
Or under yellow noons, wide waters lie
Like wrinkled bronze made hot with fires unseen.

Strange flow'rs that bloom but to an azure sun,
I saw; and all complexities of light
That work fantastic magic on the sight,
Wrought unimagined marvels one by one.

There, swifter shadows suffer gorgeous dooms—
Lost in an orange noon, an azure morn;
At twofold eve, large, winged lights are born,
Towering to meet the dawn, or briefest glooms

Of chrysoberyl filled with wondering stars,
Draw from an emerald east to skies of gold.
Tow'rd jasper waters leaning to behold,
Vague moons are lost amid great nenuphars.

Exotique

Thy mouth is like a crimson orchid-flow'r,
Whence perfume and whence poison rise unseen
To moons aswim in iris or in green,
Or mix with morning in an eastern bow'r.

Thou shouldst have known, in amaranthine isles,
The sunsets hued like fire of frankincense,
Or the long noons enfraught with redolence,
The mingled spicery of purple miles.

Thy breasts, where blood and molten marble flow,
Thy warm white limbs, thy loins of tropic snow—
These, these, by which desire is grown divine,

Were made for dreams in mystic palaces,
For love, and sleep, and slow voluptuousness,
And summer seas a-foam like foaming wine.

Desolation

It seems to me that I have lived alone—
Alone, as one that liveth in a dream:
As light on coldest marble, or the gleam
Of moons eternal on a land of stone,
The dawns have been to me. I have but known
The silence of a frozen land extreme—
A sole attending silence, all supreme
As is the sea's enormous monotone.

Upon the icy desert of my days,
No bright mirages are, but iron rays
Of dawn relentless, and the bitter light
Of all-revealing noon. Alone, I crave
The friendly clasp of finite arms, to save
My spirit from the ravening Infinite.

Crepuscle

The sunset-gonfalons are furled
On plains of evening, broad and pale,
And, wov'n athwart the waning world,
The air is like a silver veil.

Into the thin and trembling gloom,
That holds a hueless warp of light,
The murmuring wind on a slow loom,
Weaves the rich purples of the night.

A Fragment

Autumn far-off in memory,
That saw the crisping myrtles fade!
Aeons agone, my tomb was made,
Beside the moon-constrainèd sea.

Ah, wonderful its portals were!
With carven doors of chrysolite,
And walls of sombre syenite,
They wrought mine olden sepulchre!

About the griffin-guarded plinth,
White blossoms crowned the scarlet vine;
And burning orchids opaline
Illumed the palm and terebinth.

On friezes of mine ancient fame,
The cypress wrought its writhen shade;
And through the boughs the ocean made
Moresques of blue and fretted flame.

Poet or prince, I may not know
My perished name, nor bring to mind
Years that are one with dust and wind,
Nor songless love, and tongueless woe—:

Only the tomb they made for me,
With carven doors of chrysolite,
And walls of sombre syenite,
Beside the moon-constrainèd sea.

The Orchid

Beauty, thou orchid of immortal bloom,
Sprung from the fire and dust of perished spheres,
How art thou tall in these autumnal years
With the red rain of immemorial doom,
And fragrant where but lesser suns illume,
For sustenance of Life's forgotten tears!
Ever thy splendour and thy light appears
Like dawn from out the midnight of the tomb.

Colours, and gleams, and glamours unrecalled,
Richly thy petals intricate revive:
Blossom, whose roots are in Eternity,
The faithful soul, the sentience darkly thralled,
In dream and wonder evermore shall strive
At Edens lost of time and memory.

Inferno

Grey hells, or hells aglow with hot and scarlet
                                        flow'rs;
White hells of light and clamour; hells the
                                        abomination
Of breathless, deep sepulchral desolation
Oppresses ever—I have known them all, through
                                        hours
Tedious as dead eternity; where timeless pow'rs,
Leagued in malign, omnipotent persuasion—
Wearing the guise of love, despair and aspiration,
Forever drove, through ashen fields and burning
                                        bow'rs,

My soul that found no sanctuary. For Lucifer,
And all the weary, proud, imperious, baffled ones
Made in his image, hell is anywhere: The ice
Of hyperboreal deserts, or the blowing spice
In winds from off Sumatra, for each wanderer
Preserves the jealous flame of sad, infernal suns.

Mirrors

Mirrors of steel or silver, gold or glass antique!
Whether in melancholy marble palaces
In some long trance you drew the dreamy
       loveliness
Of Roman queens, or queens barbarical, or Greek;
Or, further than the bright and sun-pursuing beak
Of argosy might fare, beheld the empresses
Of lost Lemuria; or behind the lattices
Alhambran, have returned forbidden smiles
       oblique

Of wan, mysterious women!—Mirrors, mirrors
       old,
Mirrors immutable, impassable as Fate,
Your bosoms held the perished beauty of the past
Nearer than straining love might ever hope to
       hold;
And fleeing faces, lips too phantom-frail to last,
Found in your magic depth a life re-duplicate.

Belated Love

Ah, woe is me, for Love hath lain asleep,
Hath lain too long in some Morphean close,—
Till on his dreaming wings the ruined rose
Fell lightly, and the rose-red leaves were deep.

Alas, alas, for Love is overlate!
Far-wandering, alone, we know not where,
He found the white and purple poppies fair,
Nor heard the Summer pass importunate.

Ah, Love, can we forgive thy loitering?
The golden Summer, as a dream foregone
Is changed—till in our eyes the ashen dawn
Of Autumn kindles. We have heard thy wing
But with a sound of sighing; heart on heart,
In our own sighs we hear thy wing depart.

The Absence of the Muse

O, Muse, where lingerest thou? In any land
Of Saturn, lit with moons and nenuphars?
Or in what high metropolis of Mars—
Hearing the gongs of dire, occult command,
And bugles blown from strand to unknown strand
Of continents embattled in old wars
That primal kings began? Or on the bars
Of ebbing seas in Venus, from the sand
Of shattered nacre with a thousand hues,
Dost pluck the blossoms of the purple wrack
And roses of blue coral for thy hair?
Or, flown beyond the roaring Zodiac,
Translatest thou the tale of earthly news
And earthly songs to singers of Altair?

Dissonance

The harsh, brief sob of broken horns; the sound
Of hammers, on some echoing sepulchre;
Lutes in a thunderstorm; a dulcimer
By sudden drums and clamouring bugles drowned;
Crackle of pearls, and gritting rubies, ground
Beneath an iron heel; the heavy whirr
Of battle wheels; a hungry leopard's purr,
And sigh of swords withdrawing from the
wound—:

All, all are in thy dreadful fugue, O Life,
Thy dark, malign and monstrous music, spun
In hell, from a delirious Satan's dream!
O! dissonance primordial and supreme—
The moan, the thunder, evermore at strife,
Beneath the unheeding silence of the sun!

To Nora May French

Importunate, the lion-throated sea,
Blind with the mounting foam of winter, mourns
To cliffs where cling the wrenched and laboured
roots

Of cypresses, and blossoms granite-grown
Lose in the gale their tattered petals, cast
On bleak, tumultuous cauldrons of the tide,
Where fell thy molten ashes. Past the bay,
The morning dunes a dust of marble seem—
Wrought from primeval fanes to Beauty reared,
And shattered by some vandal Titan's mace
To more than Time's own ruin. Woods of pine,
Above the dunes in Gothic gloom recede,
And climb the ridge that arches to the north
Long as a lolling dragon's chine. The gulls,
Like ashen leaves far-off upon the wind,
Flutter above the broad and smouldering sea,
That lightens with the fire-white foam: But thou,
Of whom the sea is urn and sepulcher,
Who hast thereof a blown, tumultuous sleep,
And stormy peace in gulfs impacable—
What carest thou if Beauty loiter there,
Clad with the crystal noon? What carest thou
If sharp and sudden balsams of the pine
Mingle for her in the air's bright thurible
With keener fragrance proffered by the deep
From riven gulfs resounding? Knowest thou
What solemn shores of crocus-colored light,
Reared by the sunset in its realm of change,

Will mock the dream-lost isles that sirens ward,
And charm the icy emerald of the seas
To unabiding iris? Knowest thou
The waxing of the wan December foam—
A thunder-cloven veil that climbs and falls
Upon the cliffs forever?

Thou art still
As they that sleep in the eldest pyramid—
Or mounded with Mesopotamia
And immemorial deserts! Thou hast part
In the wordless, dumb conspiracy of death—
Silence wherein the warrior kings accord,
And all the wrangling sages! If thy voice
In any wise return, and word of thee,
It is a lost, incognizable sigh,
Upon the wind's oblivious woe, or blown,
Antiphonal, from wave to plangent wave
In the vast, unhuman sorrow of the main,
On tides that lave the city-laden shores
Of lands wherein the eternal vanities
Are served at many altars; tides that wash
Lemuria's unfathomable walls,
And idly sway the weed-involvèd oars
At wharves of lost Atlantis; tides that rise
From coral-coffered bones of all the drowned,
And sunless tombs of pearl that krakens guard.

As none shall roam the sad Leucadian rock,
Above the sea's immitigable moan,
But in his heart a song that Sappho sang,

And flame-like murmur of the muted lyres
That time hath not extinguished, and the cry
Of nightingales two thousand years ago,
Shall mix with those remorseful chords that break
To endless foam and thunder; and he learn
The unsleeping woe that lives in Mytelene
Till wave and deep are dumb with ice, and rime
Hath paled the rose forever—even thus,
Daughter of Sappho, passion-souled and fair,
Whose face the lutes of Lesbos would have sung,
And white Errina followed—even thus,
The western wave is eloquent of thee,
And half the wine-like fragrance of the foam
Is attar of thy spirit, and the pines
From breasts of mournful, melancholy green,
Release remembered echoes of thy song
To airs importunate. No wraith of fog,
Twice-ghostly with the Hecatean moon,
Nor rack of blown, fantasmal spume shall rise,
But I will dream thy spirit walks the sea,
Unpacified with Lethe. Thou art grown
A part of all sad beauty, and my soul
Hath found thy buried sorrow in its own,
Inseparable forever. Moons that pass,
Immaculate, to solemn pyres of snow,
And meres whereon the broken lotus dies,
Are kin to thee, as wine-lipped autumn is,
With suns of swift, irreparable change,
And lucid evenings eager-starred. Of thee,
The pearlèd fountains tell, and winds that take
In one white swirl the petals of the plum,
And leave the branches lonely. Royal blooms
Of the magnolia, pale as Beauty's brow,

And foam-white myrtles, and the fiery, bright
Pome-granate flow'rs, will subtly speak of thee
While spring hath speech and meaning. Music

hath

Her fugitive and uncommanded chords,
That thrill with tremors of thy mystery,
Or turn the void thy fleeing soul hath left
To murmurs inenarrable, that hold
Epiphanies of blind, conceiveless vision,
And things we dare not know, and dare not

dream.

Note: Nora May French, the most gifted poet of
her sex that America has produced, died by her own
hand at Carmel in 1907. Her ashes were strewn into
the sea from Point Lobos.

Recompense

Ah, more to me than many days and many dreams
And more than every hope, or any memory,
This moment, when thy lips are laid immortally
On mine, and death and time are shadows of old

dreams.

Now all the crownless, ruined years have

recompense:
In one supreme, undying hour of light and fire,
The many moons and suns have found their one

desire—
When in the hour of love, all life has recompense.

Transcendence

To look on love with disenamoured eyes;
To see with gaze relentless, rendered clear
Of hope or hatred, of desire and fear,
The insuperable nullity that lies
Behind the veils of various disguise
Which life or death may haply weave; to hear
Forevermore in flute and harp the mere
And all-resolving silence; recognize
The gules of autumn in the greening leaf,
And in the poppy-pod the poppy-flow'r—
This is to be the lord of love and grief,
O'er Time's illusion and thyself supreme,
As, half-aroused in some nocturnal hour,
The dreamer knows and dominates his dream.

Satiety

Dear you were as is the tree of Being
To the happy dead in heaven's bow'rs.
Whence and what, this evil spell that flings me
Forth from love with loveless eyes unseeing?

Fair you were as nymph or queen of vision—
Bosomed like the succubi of dreams.
All your beauty turns to sad, ironic
Weariness, and sorrowful derision.

Lo, of what avail our spent caresses,—
Kisses that set the summer night aflame?
Mute, enormous languor without cause—
What is this my autumn heart confesses?

All your breast was fragrant like the flowers
Of the grape on hills toward the south.
Love is acrid now like staling asters,
Sodden with the rain of autumn hours.

The Ministers of Law

The glories and the perils of thy day
Are one, O Man! Thou goest to thine end
With Pow'rs, and for a little thou dost wend
With marshalled Majesties upon their way:
But thee the dread Necessities betray
That nurse, and fearful Splendours that befriend;
And thee shall alien Dominations rend.
Deemest the triumph of the worlds to stay,
Or step by step eternal, unsurpassed,
Stride with the suns upon their road of awe?
Thou travelest brief ways that end and sink—
Urged by the hurrying planets; and the vast,
Prone-rushing constellations of the Law,
Thunder and press behind thee at the brink.

Coldness

Thy heart will not believe in love:
Therefore is love become to me
A dream, an empty mockery,
And death and life are less than love.

O, bright and beautiful as flame
Thy hair, and pale thy lips, and eyes
Like seas wherein the waning skies
Of autumn lie in paler flame.

Forevermore thy heart abides,
A dreaming crystal, pure and cold,
Amid whose visions manifold
No shape nor any shade abides.

Thy days are void and vain as death:
The moons and morrows weave for thee
A sleep of light eternally,
Where life is as a dream of death.

Chill as white jewels, or the moon,
And virginal as ice or fire,
Thou knowest life and life's desire
As a bright mirror knows the moon.

Lo, if thy heart believed in love,
It were not more nor less to me:
I know THY love a mockery,
And all my dreams less vain than love.

Song

I bring my weariness to thee,
My bitter dreams I bring;
Love with a wounded wing,
And life consumed of memory,
I bring to thee.

The haven of thy happy breast—
Of this my dreams are fain:
For all my weary pain,
In all the world there is no rest,
But on thy breast.

The Desert Garden

Dreaming, I said, "When she is come,
This desert garden that is me,
For her shall offer mellowly
Its myrrh and its olibanum—
When she is come.

"The flowers of the moon for her,
With blossoms of the sun shall bloom,
The fading roses breathe perfume,
The lightly fallen petals stir,
And sigh to her.
"Her presence, like a living wind
Each little leaf makes visible,
Shall enter there, or like the spell
(Upon the lulling leaves divined)
Of silent wind."

Alas! for she is come and gone,
And in the garden, green for her,
The flowers fall, the flowers stir
Only to winds of night and dawn:
For she is gone.

The Crucifixion of Eros

Because of thee, immortal Love hath died:
Because thy wilful heart will not believe,
Thy hands and mine a thorny crown must weave,
A thorny crown for Love the crucified.

Behold, how beautiful the limbs that bleed—
The limbs that bleed, O stubborn heart, for us!
Still are the lids so softly tremulous,
And mute the mouth of our eternal need.

Though this thy fearful lips would now deny,
Love is divine, and cannot wholly die:
Draw forth the nails thy tender hands have
                                        driven—

And we will know the mercy infinite,
Will find redemption in our own delight,
And in each other's heart the only heaven.

The Exile

Against my heart your heart is closed; you bid me
go:
What ways are left in all the world for Love to
know?
Desolate oceans, and the light of lonely plains,
Dead moons that wander in the wastes of ice and
snow—

These, these I fain would see, and find the
splendid bourne
Of sunset, or the brazen deserts of the morn,
That I might lose this ever-aching loneliness
In vaster solitude; and love be less forlorn,

Faring to seek with alien sun and alien star
The strange, the veiled horizons infinite and far;
Spaces of fire and night, the skies of steel and
gold,
Or sunset-haunted seas where foamless islands
are.

Ave Atque Vale

Black dreams; the pale and sorrowful desire
Whose eyes have looked on Lethe, and have seen,
Deep in the sliding ebon tide serene,
Their own vain light inverted; ashen fire,
With wasted lilies, late and languishing;
Autumnal roses blind with rain; slow foam
From desert-sinking seas, with honeycomb
Of aconite and poppy—these I bring
With this my bitter, barren love to thee;
And from the grievous springs of memory,
Far in the great Maremma of my heart,
I proffer thee to drink; and on thy mouth,
With the one kiss wherein we meet and part,
Leave fire and dust from quenchless leagues of
drouth.

Solution

The ghostly fire that walks the fen,
Tonight thine only light shall be;
On lethal ways thy soul shall pass,
And prove the stealthy, coiled morass,
With mocking mists for company.

On roads thou goest not again,
To shores where thou hast never gone,—
Fare onward, though the shuddering queach
And serpent-rippled waters reach
Like seepage-pools of Acheron,

Beside thee; and the twisten reeds,
Close-raddled as a witch's net,
Enwind thy knees, and cling and clutch
Like wreathing adders; though the touch
Of the blind air be dank and wet,

As from a wounded Thing that bleeds
In cloud and darkness overhead—
Fare onward, where thy dreams of yore
In splendour drape the fetid shore
And pestilential waters dead.

And though the toads' irrision rise,
As grinding of Satanic racks,
And spectral willows, gaunt and grey,
Gibber along thy shrouded way,
Where vipers lie with livid backs,

And watch thee with their sulphurous eyes,—
Fare onward, till thy feet shall slip
Deep in the sudden pool ordained,
And all the noisome draught be drained,
That turns to Lethe on the lip.

The Infinite Quest

In years no vision shall aver,
In lands no dream may name,
Tow'rd alien things what longings were,
And thence what languors came!

For each horizon straightly sought,
With fealty to the stars,
What death and weariness were bought,
What bitterness, what bars!

I waken unto years afar,
And find the quest made new
In Earth, that was perchance a star
Unto my former view.

The Tears of Lilith

O lovely demon, half-divine!
Hemlock, and hydromel, and gall,
Honey, and aconite, and wine,
Mingle to make that mouth of thine—

Thy mouth I love: But most of all,
It is thy tears that I desire—
Thy tears, like fountain-drops that fall
In gardens red, Satanical;

Or like the tears of mist and fire,
Wept by the moon, that wizards use
To secret runes, when they require
Some silver philtre, sweet and dire.

A Precept

With words of ivory,
Of bronze, of ebony,
Of alabaster, marble, steel, and gold,
The beauty of the visible is told.

But how with these express
The unseen Loveliness—
Splendour and light, and harmony, and sound,
The heart hath felt, the sense hath never found?

No shining words of stone—
Shadow and cloud alone—
These shall the poet seek eternally,
Whose lines would carve the mask of Mystery.

Remembered Light

The years are a falling of snow,
Slow, but without cessation,
On hills, and mountains, and flowers and worlds
                                    that were;
But snow, and the crawling night wherein it fell,
May be washed away in one swifter hour of flame:
Thus it was that some slant of sunset
In the chasms of pilèd cloud—
Transient mountains that made a new horizon,
Uplifting the west to fantastic pinnacles—
Smote warm in a buried realm of the spirit,
Till the snows of forgetfulness were gone.
Clear in the vistas of memory,
The peaks of a world long unremembered,
Soared further than clouds but fell not,
Based on hills that shook not nor melted
With that burden enormous, hardly to be
                                    believed.

Rent with stupendous chasms,
Full of an umber twilight,
I beheld that larger world;
Bright was the twilight, sharp like ethereal wine
Above, but low in the clefts it thickened,
Dull as with duskier tincture.
Like whimsical wings outspread but unstirring,
Flowers that seemed spirits of the twilight
That must pass with its passing—
Too fragile for day or for darkness,

Fed the dusk with more delicate hues than its
own;
Stars that were nearer, more radiant than ours,
Quivered and pulsed in the clear thin gold of the
sky.

These things I beheld
Till the gold was shaken with flight
Of fantastical wings like broken shadows,
Forerunning the darkness;
Till the twilight shivered with outcry of eldritch
voices
Like pain's last cry ere oblivion.

In Lemuria

Rememberest thou? Enormous gongs of stone
Were stricken, and the storming trumpeteers
Acclaimed my deed to answering tides of spears,
And spoke the names of monsters overthrown—
Griffins whose angry gold, and fervid store
Of sapphires wrenched from marble-plungèd
mines—
Carnelians, opals, agates, almandines,
I brought to thee some scarlet eve of yore.
In the wide fane that shrined thee, Venus-wise,
The fallen clamours died. I heard the tune
Of tiny bells of pearl and melanite,
Hung at thy knees, and arms of dreamt delight;
And placed my wealth before thy fabled eyes,
Pallid and pure as jaspers from the moon.

Haunting

There is no peace amid the moonlight and the
                                        pines;
Deep in the windless gloom the lamplike thought
                                        of you
Abides; and ah, what burning memories pursue
My heart among the pallid marbles! Night assigns

Your silver face for wardress of the doors of Sleep;
Beyond the wild, last bourn of dreamland, lo, your
                                        eyes
Are on the lonesome, ultimate, undiscovered
                                        skies;
Moonlike and dim, you wander ever in the deep

Which is the secret, innermost, unknown abyss
Of my own soul, and in its night your spirit lives.
Shall I not find the very draught that Lethe gives,
Sweet with your tears, and warm with savour of
                                        your kiss?

Cleopatra

Thy beauty is the warmth and languor and passion
of a tropic autumn,

Caressing all the senses,—
With light from skies of heavy azure,
With perfume from hidden orchids many-hued
That burn in the berylline dusk of palms;
With the balmy kiss of tropic wind and wave,
And the songs of exotic birds that pass
In vermilion-flashing flight from isle to isle on a
cobalt sea.

O, sweetness in the inmost sense,
As of golden fruits that have grown by the waters
of Lethe,

Or fragrance of purple lilies, crushed by the limbs
of lovers,

In the shadow of a wood of cypress!
Thou pervadest me with thy love,
As the dawn pervadeth a valley among mountains,
Or as opaline sunset filleth the amaranth-coloured
sea;

The desire of thy heart is upon me,
As a myrtle-scented wind from the isle of Cythera,
Where Aphrodite waits for Adonis,
Lying naked among the flag lilies by a pool of
chrysolite;

I inhale thy love
As the breath of hidden gardens of purple and
scarlet,

Where Circe wanders,
Clad in a trailing gown whose colours are the gold
of flame,

And the azure of the skies of autumn.

The Hidden Paradise

Our passion is a secret Paradise—
Eden of lotos and the fruitful date,
With silence walled and held undesecrate
By man or prying seraph: We are wise

As any god and goddess, who have wrung
From roseal fruitage of a bough forbidden,
The happy wine we drink, we drink unchidden,
Deep in the vales where vernal leaves are young,

And the first poppies loiter. Though the breath
Of all the gods a bolted storm prepare,
And blood-red gloom of thunders blind the sun,

Shall we not turn, with clinging kisses there,
And, laughing, quaff some dreamless wine of
                                        death—
Triumphant still, in mere oblivion?

Ecstasy

Blind with your softly fallen hair,
I turn me from the twilight air;
And, ah, the wordless tale of love
My lips upon your lips declare!

High stars are on the shadowy south—
Unseen, unknown: The urgent drouth
Of desert years in one deep kiss,
Would drain the sweetness of your mouth.

Our straining arms that clasp and close,
Ache with an ecstasy that grows;
And passion in our secret veins,
Like burning amber, glows and glows.

This love is sweet to have and hold,
Better than sandalwood or gold,
After the barren, bitter loves,
The mad and mournful loves of old.

This love is fortunate and fair,
Behind its veil of fallen hair;
This love hath soft and clinging arms,
And a kind bosom, warm and bare.

Union

As the fumes of myrrh that mix with the odour of
                                      sandalwood
In a temple sacred to the goddess Lakme;
As moonlight mingled with starlight
In the lucent azure of an autumn lake;
As the sunset-rays of gold and crimson
That interlace on a couch of purple cloud—
Even so, Beloved,
Hath my love mingled with thine—
Even so, our souls are one,
Like two winds that meet in a valley of rose and
                                          lotus,
And fall to rest, uniting
As the still and fragrant air that lingers
On a bed of falling petals.

Psalm

My beloved is a well of clear waters,
To which I have come at noontide,
From the land of the Abomination of Desolation,
From the lion-dreaded waste,
Where nothing dwelleth but the inconsolable
crying of an evil wind,
And the wandering realms and cities of the wide
mirage;
Where no one passeth except the sun,
Who walked like a terrible god through the hell of
the brazen skies;
And the dreadful cohorts of the constellations,
Who pass remote in alien years,
And clad with icy azures of unattainable distance.

My beloved is a singing fountain,
Set in a wide oasis,
Between the frondage of the fruitful palm,
And the branches of the flowering myrtle:
The wind that bloweth thereon,
Hath lain in a vale of cassia and myrrh,
And caressed the vermilion blossoms of the
pomegranate,
Whose red is the red of the lips of Astarte;
A thousand nightingales are gathered there,
From all the gardens of lost romance;
And plots of purple and silver lillies,
More beautiful than the meadows of mirage,
Revive the flowers of Sabean queens,
And the blossoms worn by all the princesses of
legend.

Ah, suffer me to dwell
Thereby, and forget the gilded cities of desire,
The domes of spectral gold,
That fled from horizon to horizon
Before me, and left my feet in the sinking vales
and shifting plains of the desert,
Whose waters are green with corruption,
And bitter with the dust and ashes of death.
Ah, suffer me to sleep
In the balsam-laden shadows of the palm and
myrtle,
By the ever-springing fountain!

Symbols

No more of gold and marble, nor of snow,
And sunlight, and vermilion, would I make
My vision and my symbols, nor would take
The auroral flame of some prismatic floe,
Nor iris of the frail and lunar bow,
Flung on the shafted waterfalls that wake
The night's blue slumber in a shadowy lake.
To body forth my fantasies, and show
Communicable mystery, I would find,
In adamantine darkness of the earth,
Metals untouched of any sun; and bring
Black azures of the nether sea to birth—
Or fetch the secret, splendid leaves, and blind,
Blue lilies of an Atlantean spring.

In November

With autumn and the flaring leaves our love must
end—
Ere flauntful spring shall mock thy tears and my
despair
With blossoms red or pale, some April bride may
wear:
Now, while the weary, grey, forgetful heavens
bend

Above the grief and languor of the dying lands,
In one last kiss shall meet and mingle and expire
The muted, last, remembering sighs of our desire;
And on my face the flower-like burden of thy
hands

Shall rest a little, and be taken tenderly,
And, ah, how lightly hence! And in thy golden
eyes,
Thy love, and all the ashen glory of the skies,
Shall mingle, and as in a mirror lie for me.

The Hashish-Eater;

or, the Apocalypse of Evil

Bow down: I am the emperor of dreams;
I crown me with the million-coloured sun
Of secret worlds incredible, and take
Their trailing skies for vestment, when I soar,
Throned on the mounting zenith, and illume
The spaceward-flown horizons infinite.
Like rampant monsters roaring for their glut,
The fiery-crested oceans rise and rise,
By jealous moons maleficently urged
To follow me forever; mountains horned
With peaks of sharpest adamant, and mawed
With sulphur-lit volcanoes lava-langued,
Usurp the skies with thunder, but in vain;
And continents of serpent-shapen trees,
With slimy trunks that lengthen league by league,
Pursue my flight through ages spurned to fire
By that supreme ascendance. Sorcerers
And evil kings predominantly armed
With scrolls of fulvous dragon-skin, whereon
Are worm-like runes of ever-twisting flame,
Would stay me; and the sirens of the stars,
With foam-light songs from silver fragrance

                                                  wrought,

Would lure me to their crystal reefs; and moons
Where viper-eyed, senescent devils dwell,
With antic gnomes abominably wise,
Heave up their icy horns across my way:

But naught deters me from the goal ordained
By suns, and aeons, and immortal wars,
And sung by moons and motes; the goal whose

name

Is all the secret of forgotten glyphs,
By sinful gods in torrid rubies writ
For ending of a brazen book; the goal
Whereat my soaring ecstacy may stand,
In amplest heavens multiplied to hold
My hordes of thunder-vested avatars,
And Promethèan armies of my thought,
That brandish claspèd levins. There I call
My memories, intolerably clad
In light the peaks of paradise may wear,
And lead the Armageddon of my dreams,
Whose instant shout of triumph is become
Immensity's own music: For their feet
Are founded on innumerable worlds,
Remote in alien epochs, and their arms
Upraised, are columns potent to exalt
With ease ineffable the countless thrones
Of all the gods that are and gods to be,
Or bear the seats of Asmadai and Set
Above the seventh paradise.

Supreme
In culminant omniscience manifold,
And served by senses multitudinous,
Far-posted on the shifting walls of time,
With eyes that roam the star-unwinnowed fields
Of utter night and chaos, I convoke
The Babel of their visions, and attend
At once their myriad witness: I behold,

In Ombos, where the fallen Titans dwell,
With mountain-builded walls, and gulfs for moat,
The secret cleft that cunning dwarves have dug
Beneath an alp-like buttress; and I list,
Too late, the clang of adamantine gongs,
Dinned by their drowsy guardians, whose feet
Have felt the wasp-like sting of little knives,
Embrued with slobber of the basilisk,
Or juice of wounded upas. And I see,
In gardens of a crimson-litten world
The sacred flow'r with lips of purple flesh,
And silver-lashed, vermilion-lidded eyes
Of torpid azure; whom his furtive priests
At moonless eve in terror seek to slay,
With bubbling grails of sacrificial blood
That hide a hueless poison. And I read,
Upon the tongue of a forgotten sphinx,
The annuling word a spiteful demon wrote
With gall of slain chimeras; and I know
What pentacles the lunar wizards use,
That once allured the gulf-returning roc,
With ten great wings of furlèd storm, to pause
Midmost an alabaster mount; and there,
With boulder-weighted webs of dragons'-gut,
Uplift by cranes a captive giant built,
They wound the monstrous, moonquake-
                                    throbbing bird,
And plucked, from off his sabre-taloned feet,
Uranian sapphires fast in frozen blood,
With amethysts from Mars. I lean to read,
With slant-lipped mages, in an evil star,
The monstrous archives of a war that ran
Through wasted aeons, and the prophecy

Of wars renewed, that shall commemorate
Some enmity of wivern-headed kings,
Even to the brink of time. I know the blooms
Of bluish fungus, freaked with mercury,
That bloat within the craters of the moon,
And in one still, selenic hour have shrunk
To pools of slime and fetor; and I know
What clammy blossoms, blanched and cavern-

                           grown,

Are proffered in Uranus to their gods
By mole-eyed peoples; and the livid seed
Of some black fruit a king in Saturn ate,
Which, cast upon his tinkling palace-floor,
Took root between the burnished flags, and now
Hath mounted, and become a hellish tree,
Whose lithe and hairy branches, lined with

                           mouths,

Net like a hundred ropes his lurching throne,
And strain at starting pillars. I behold
The slowly-thronging corals, that usurp
Some harbour of a million-masted sea,
And sun them on the league-long wharves of

                           gold—

Bulks of enormous crimson, kraken-limbed
And kraken-headed, lifting up as crowns
The octiremes of perished emperors,
And galleys fraught with royal gems, that sailed
From a sea-deserted haven.

Swifter grow
The visions: Now a mighty city looms,
Hewn from a hill of purest cinnabar,
To domes and turrets like a sunrise thronged

With tier on tier of captive moons, half-drowned
In shifting erubescence. But whose hands
Were sculptors of its doors, and columns wrought
To semblance of prodigious blooms of old,
No eremite hath lingered there to say,
And no man comes to learn: For long ago
A prophet came, warning its timid king
Against the plague of lichens that had crept
Across subverted empires, and the sand
Of wastes that Cyclopean mountains ward;
Which, slow and ineluctable, would come,
To take his fiery bastions and his fanes,
And quench his domes with greenish tetter. Now
I see a host of naked giants, armed
With horns of behemoth and unicorn,
Who wander, blinded by the clinging spells
Of hostile wizardry, and stagger on
To forests where the very leaves have eyes,
And ebonies like wrathful dragons roar
To teaks a-chuckle in the loathly gloom;
Where coiled lianas lean, with serried fangs,
From writhing palms with swollen boles that

                                moan;

Where leeches of a scarlet moss have sucked
The eyes of some dead monster, and have crawled
To bask upon his azure-spotted spine;
Where hydra-throated blossoms hiss and sing,
Or yawn with mouths that drip a sluggish dew,
Whose touch is death and slow corrosion. Then,
I watch a war of pigmies, met by night,
With pitter of their drums of parrot's hide,
On plains with no horizon, where a god
Might lose his way for centuries; and there,

In wreathèd light, and fulgors all convolved,
A rout of green, enormous moons ascend,
With rays that like a shivering venom run
On inch-long swords of lizard-fang.

Surveyed
From this my throne, as from a central sun,
The pageantries of worlds and cycles pass;
Forgotten splendours, dream by dream unfold,
Like tapestry, and vanish; violet suns,
Or suns of changeful iridescence, bring
Their rays about me, like the coloured lights
Imploring priests might lift to glorify
The face of some averted god; the songs
Of mystic poets in a purple world,
Ascend to me in music that is made
From unconceivèd perfumes, and the pulse
Of love ineffable; the lute-players
Whose lutes are strung with gold of the utmost
                                        moon,
Call forth delicious languors, never known
Save to their golden kings; the sorcerers
Of hooded stars inscrutable to God,
Surrender me their demon-wrested scrolls,
Inscribed with lore of monstrous alchemies,
And awful transformations. If I will,
I am at once the vision and the seer,
And mingle with my ever-streaming pomps,
And still abide their suzerain: I am
The neophyte who serves a nameless god,
Within whose fane the fanes of Hecatompylos
Were arks the Titan worshippers might bear,
Or flags to pave the threshold; or I am

The god himself, who calls the fleeing clouds
Into the nave where suns might congregate,
And veils the darkling mountain of his face
With fold on solemn fold; for whom the priests
Amass their monthly hecatomb of gems—
Opals that are a camel-cumbering load,
And monstrous alabraundines, won from war
With realms of hostile serpents; which arise,
Combustible, in vapours many-hued,
And myrrh-excelling perfumes. It is I,
The king, who holds with scepter-dropping hand
The helm of some great barge of chrysolite,
Sailing upon an amethystine sea
To isles of timeless summer: For the snows
Of hyperborean winter, and their winds,
Sleep in his jewel-builded capital,
Nor any charm of flame-wrought wizardry,
Nor conjured suns may rout them; so he flees,
With captive kings to urge his serried oars,
Hopeful of dales where amaranthine dawn
Hath never left the faintly sighing lote
And fields of lisping moly. Or I fare,
Impanoplied with azure diamond,
As hero of a quest Achernar lights,
To deserts filled with ever-wandering flames,
That feed upon the sullen marl, and soar
To wrap the slopes of mountains, and to leap,
With tongues intolerably lengthening,
That lick the blenchèd heavens. But there lives
(Secure as in a garden walled from wind)
A lonely flower by a placid well,
Midmost the flaring tumult of the flames,
That roar as roars the storm-possessèd sea,

Implacable forever: And within
That simple grail the blossom lifts, there lies
One drop of an incomparable dew,
Which heals the parchèd weariness of kings,
And cures the wound of wisdom. I am page
To an emperor who reigns ten thousand years,
And through his labyrinthine palace-rooms,
Through courts and colonnades and balconies
Wherein immensity itself is mazed,
I seek the golden gorget he hath lost,
On which the names of his conniving stars
Are writ in little sapphires; and I roam
For centuries, and hear the brazen clocks
Innumerably clang with such a sound
As brazen hammers make, by devils dinned
On tombs of all the dead; and nevermore
I find the gorget, but at length I find
A sealèd room whose nameless prisoner
Moans with a nameless torture, and would turn
To hell's red rack as to a lilied couch
From that whereon they stretched him; and I find,
Prostrate upon a lotus-painted floor,
The loveliest of all beloved slaves
My emperor hath, and from her pulseless side
A serpent rises, whiter than the root
Of some venefic bloom in darkness grown,
And gazes up with green-lit eyes that seem
Like drops of cold, congealing poison.

Hark!
What word was whispered in a tongue unknown,
In crypts of some impenetrable world?
Whose is the dark, dethroning secrecy

I cannot share, though I am king of suns
And king therewith of strong eternity,
Whose gnomons with their swords of shadow
                                            guard
My gates, and slay the intruder? Silence loads
The wind of ether, and the worlds are still
To hear the word that flees me. All my dreams
Fall like a rack of fuming vapours raised
To semblance by a necromant, and leave
Spirit and sense unthinkably alone,
Above a universe of shrouded stars,
And suns that wander, cowled with sullen gloom,
Like witches to a Sabbath. Fear is born
In crypts below the nadir, and hath crawled
Reaching the floor of space and waits for wings
To lift it upward, like a hellish worm
Fain for the flesh of seraphs. Eyes that gleam,
But are not eyes of suns or galaxies,
Gather and throng to the base of darkness; flame
Behind some black, abysmal curtain burns,
Implacable, and fanned to whitest wrath
By raisèd wings that flail the whiffled gloom,
And make a brief and broken wind that moans,
As one who rides a throbbing rack. There is
A Thing that crouches, worlds and years remote,
Whose horns a demon sharpens, rasping forth
A note to shatter the donjon-keeps of time,
And crack the sphere of crystal. All is dark
For ages, and my tolling heart suspends
Its clamour, as within the clutch of death,
Tightening with tense, hermetic rigours. Then,
In one enormous, million-flashing flame,
The stars unveil, the suns remove their cowls,

And beam to their responding planets; time
Is mine once more, and armies of its dreams
Rally to that insuperable throne,
Firmed on the central zenith.

Now I seek
The meads of shining moly I had found
In some remoter vision, by a stream
No cloud hath ever tarnished; where the sun,
A gold Narcissus, loiters evermore
Above his golden image: But I find
A corpse the ebbing water will not keep,
With eyes like sapphires that have lain in hell,
And felt the hissing embers; and the flow'rs
About me turn to hooded serpents, swayed
By flutes of devils in a hellish dance,
Meet for the nod of Satan, when he reigns
Above the raging Sabbath, and is wooed
By sarabands of witches. But I turn
To mountains guarding with their horns of snow
The source of that befoulèd rill, and seek
A pinnacle where none but eagles climb,
And they with failing pennons. But in vain
I flee, for on that pylon of the sky,
Some curse hath turned the unprinted snow to
flame—
Red fires that curl and cluster to my tread,
Trying the summit's narrow cirque. And now,
I see a silver python far beneath—
Vast as a river that a fiend hath witched,
And forced to flow remèant in its course
To fountains whence it issued. Rapidly
It winds from slope to crumbling slope, and fills

Ravines and chasmal gorges, till the crags
Totter with coil on coil incumbent. Soon
It hath entwined the pinnacle I keep,
And gapes with a fanged, unfathomable maw,
Wherein great Typhon, and Enceladus,
Were orts of daily glut. But I am gone,
For at my call a hippogriff hath come,
And firm between his thunder-beating wings,
I mount the sheer cerulean walls of noon,
And see the earth, a spurnèd pebble, fall
Lost in the fields of nether stars—and seek
A planet where the outwearied wings of time
Might pause and furl for respite, or the plumes
Of death be stayed, and loiter in reprieve
Above some deathless lily: For therein,
Beauty hath found an avatar of flow'rs—
Blossoms that clothe it as a coloured flame,
From peak to peak, from pole to sullen pole,
And turn the skies to perfume. There I find
A lonely castle, calm and unbeset,
Save by the purple spears of amaranth,
And tender-sworded iris. Walls upbuilt
Of flushèd marble, wonderful with rose,
And domes like golden bubbles, and minarets
That take the clouds as coronal—these are mine,
For voiceless looms the peaceful barbican,
And the heavy-teethed portcullis hangs aloft
As if to smile a welcome. So I leave
My hippogriff to crop the magic meads,
And pass into a court the lilies hold,
And tread them to a fragrance that pursues
To win the portico, whose columns, carved
Of lazuli and amber, mock the palms

Of bright, Aidennic forests—capitalled
With fronds of stone fretted to airy lace,
Enfolding drupes that seem as tawny clusters
Of breasts of unknown houris; and convolved
With vines of shut and shadowy-leavèd flow'rs,
Like the dropt lids of women that endure
Some loin-dissolving rapture. Through a door
Enlaid with lilies twined luxuriously,
I enter, dazed and blinded with the sun,
And hear, in gloom that changing colours cloud,
A chuckle sharp as crepitating ice,
Upheaved and cloven by shoulders of the damned
Who strive in Antenora. When my eyes
Undazzle, and the cloud of colour fades,
I find me in a monster-guarded room,
Where marble apes with wings of griffins crowd
On walls an evil sculptor wrought, and beasts
Wherein the sloth and vampire-bat unite,
Pendulous by their toes of tarnished bronze,
Usurp the shadowy interval of lamps
That hang from ebon arches. Like a ripple,
Borne by the wind from pool to sluggish pool
In fields where wide Cocytus flows his bound,
A crackling smile around that circle runs,
And all the stone-wrought gibbons stare at me
With eyes that turn to glowing coals. A fear
That found no name in Babel, flings me on,
Breathless and faint with horror, to a hall
Within whose weary, self-reverting round,
The languid curtains, heavier than palls,
Unnumerably depict a weary king,
Who fain would cool his jewel-crusted hands
In lakes of emerald evening, or the fields

Of dreamless poppies pure with rain. I flee
Onward, and all the shadowy curtains shake
With tremors of a silken-sighing mirth,
And whispers of the innumerable king,
Breathing a tale of ancient pestilence,
Whose very words are vile contagion. Then
I reach a room where caryatids,
Carved in the form of tall, voluptuous Titan

women,

Surround a throne of flowering ebony
Where creeps a vine of crystal. On the throne,
There lolls a wan, enormous Worm, whose bulk,
Tumid with all the rottenness of kings,
O'erflows its arms with fold on creasèd fold
Of fat obscenely bloating. Open-mouthed
He leans, and from his throat a score of tongues,
Depending like to wreaths of torpid vipers,
Drivel with phosphorescent slime, that runs
Down all his length of soft and monstrous folds,
And creeping among the flow'rs of ebony,
Lends them the life of tiny serpents. Now,
Ere the Horror ope those red and lashless slits
Of eyes that draw the gnat and midge, I turn,
And follow down a dusty hall, whose gloom,
Lined by the statues with their mighty limbs,
Ends in a golden-roofed balcony
Sphering the flowered horizon.

Ere my heart
Hath hushed the panic tumult of its pulses,
I listen, from beyond the horizon's rim,
A mutter faint as when the far simoon,
Mounting from unknown deserts, opens forth,

Wide as the waste, those wings of torrid night
That fling the doom of cities from their folds,
And musters in its van a thousand winds,
That with disrooted palms for besoms, rise
And sweep the sands to fury. As the storm,
Approaching, mounts and loudens to the ears
Of them that toil in fields of sesame,
So grows the mutter, and a shadow creeps
Above the gold horizon, like a dawn
Of darkness climbing sunward. Now they come,
A Sabbath of abominable shapes,
Led by the fiends and lamiae of worlds
That owned my sway aforetime! Cockatrice,
Python, tragelaphus, leviathan,
Chimera, martichoras, behemoth,
Geryon and sphinx, and hydra, on my ken
Arise as might some Afrite-builded city,
Consummate in the lifting of a lash,
With thundrous domes and sounding obelisks,
And towers of night and fire alternate! Wings
Of white-hot stone along the hissing wind,
Bear up the huge and furnace-hearted beasts
Of hells beyond Rutilicus; and things
Whose lightless length would mete the gyre of
                                          moons—
Born from the caverns of a dying sun,
Uncoil to the very zenith, half disclosed
From gulfs below the horizon; octopi
Like blazing moons with countless arms of fire,
Climb from the seas of ever-surging flame
That roll and roar through planets unconsumed,
Beating on coasts of unknown metals; beasts
That range the mighty worlds of Alioth, rise,

Aforesting the heavens with multitudinous horns,
Within whose maze the winds are lost; and borne
On cliff-like brows of plunging scolopendras,
The shell-wrought tow'rs of ocean-witches loom,
And griffin-mounted gods, and demons throned
On sable dragons, and the cockodrills
That bear the spleenful pygmies on their backs;
And blue-faced wizards from the worlds of Saiph,
On whom Titanic scorpions fawn; and armies
That move with fronts reverted from the foe,
And strike athwart their shoulders at the shapes
Their shields reflect in crystal; and eidola
Fashioned within unfathomable caves
By hands of eyeless peoples; and the blind
And worm-shaped monsters of a sunless world,
With krakens from the ultimate abyss,
And Demogorgons of the outer dark,
Arising, shout with multitudinous thunders,
And threatening me with dooms ineffable
In words whereat the heavens leap to flame,
Advance on the magic palace! Thrown before,
For league on league, their blasting shadows

                          blight

And eat like fire the amaranthine meads,
Leaving an ashen desert! In the palace,
I hear the apes of marble shriek and howl.
And all the women-shapen columns moan,
Babbling with unknown terror. In my fear,
A monstrous dread unnamed in any hell,
I rise, and flee with the fleeing wind for wings,
And in a trice the magic palace reels,
And spiring to a single tow'r of flame,
Goes out, and leaves nor shard nor ember! Flown

Beyond the world, upon that fleeing wind,
I reach the gulf's irrespirable verge,
Where fails the strongest storm for breath and

                                     fall,

Supportless, through the nadir-plunged gloom,
Beyond the scope and vision of the sun,
To other skies and systems. In a world
Deep-wooded with the multi-coloured fungi,
That soar to semblance of fantastic palms,
I fall as falls the meteor-stone, and break
A score of trunks to powder. All unhurt,
I rise, and through the illimitable woods,
Among the trees of flimsy opal, roam,
And see their tops that clamber, hour by hour,
To touch the suns of iris. Things unseen,
Whose charnel breath informs the tideless air
With spreading pools of fetor, follow me
Elusive past the ever-changing palms;
And pittering moths, with wide and ashen wings,
Flit on before, and insects ember-hued,
Descending, hurtle through the gorgeous gloom,
And quench themselves in crumbling thickets.

                                            Heard

Far-off, the gong-like roar of beasts unknown
Resounds at measured intervals of time,
Shaking the riper trees to dust, that falls
In clouds of acrid perfume, stifling me
Beneath a pall of iris.

Now the palms
Grow far apart and lessen momently
To shrubs a dwarf might topple. Over them
I see an empty desert, all ablaze

With amethysts and rubies, and the dust
Of garnets or carnelians. On I roam,
Treading the gorgeous grit, that dazzles me
With leaping waves of endless rutilance,
Whereby the air is turned to a crimson gloom,
Through which I wander, blind as any Kobold;
Till underfoot the griding sands give place
To stone or metal, with a massive ring
More welcome to mine ears than golden bells,
Or tinkle of silver fountains. When the gloom
Of crimson lifts, I stand upon the edge
Of a broad black plain of adamant, that reaches,
Level as a windless water, to the verge
Of all the world; and through the sable plain,
A hundred streams of shattered marble run,
And streams of broken steel, and streams of
                                  bronze,
Like to the ruin of all the wars of time,
To plunge, with clangour of timeless cataracts,
Adown the gulfs eternal.

So I follow,
Between a river of steel and a river of bronze,
With ripples loud and tuneless as the clash
Of a million lutes; and come to the precipice
From which they fall, and make the mighty sound
Of a million swords that meet a million shields,
Or din of spears and armour in the wars
Of all the worlds and aeons: Far beneath,
They fall, through gulfs and cycles of the void,
And vanish like a stream of broken stars,
Into the nether darkness; nor the gods
Of any sun, nor demons of the gulf,

Will dare to know what everlasting sea
Is fed thereby, and mounts forevermore
With mighty tides unebbing.

Lo, what cloud,
Or night of sudden and supreme eclipse,
Is on the suns of opal? At my side,
The rivers rail with a wan and ghostly gleam,
Through darkness falling as the night that falls
From mighty spheres extinguished! Turning now,
I see, betwixt the desert and the suns,
The poised wings of all the dragon-rout,
Far-flown in black occlusion thousand-fold
Through stars, and deeps, and devastated worlds,
Upon my trail of terror! Griffins, rocs,
And sluggish, dark chimeras, heavy-winged
After the ravin of dispeopled lands,
With harpies, and the vulture-birds of hell—
Hot from abominable feasts and fain
To cool their beaks and talons in my blood—
All, all have gathered, and the wingless rear,
With rank on rank of foul, colossal Worms,
Like pillars of embattled night and flame,
Looms on the wide horizon! From the van,
I hear the shriek of wyvers, loud and shrill
As tempests in a broken fane, and roar
Of sphinxes, like the unrelenting toll
Of bells from tow'rs infernal. Cloud on cloud,
They arch the zenith, and a dreadful wind
Falls from them like the wind before the storm.
And in the wind my cloven garment streams,
And flutters in the face of all the void,
Even as flows a flaffing spirit, lost

On the Pit's undying tempest! Louder grows
The thunder of the streams of stone and
                                    bronze.—
Redoubled with the roar of torrent wings,
Inseparably mingled. Scarce I keep
My footing, in the gulfward winds of fear,
And mighty thunders, beating to the void
In sea-like waves incessant; and would flee
With them, and prove the nadir-founded night
Where fall the streams of ruin; but when I reach
The verge, and seek through sun-defeating gloom,
To measure with my gaze the dread descent,
I see a tiny star within the depths—
A light that stays me, while the wings of doom
Convene their thickening thousands: For the star
Increases, taking to its hueless orb,
With all the speed of horror-changèd dreams
The light as of a million million moons;
And floating up through gulfs and glooms eclipsed,
It grows and grows, a huge white eyeless Face,
That fills the void and fills the universe,
And bloats against the limits of the world
With lips of flame that open.

The Sorrow of the Winds

O winds that pass uncomforted
Through all the peacefulness of spring,
And tell the trees your sorrowing,
That they must mourn till ye are fled!

Think ye the Tyrian distance holds
The crystal of unquestioned sleep?
That those forgetful purples keep
No veiled, contentious greens and golds?

Half with communicated grief,
Half that they are not free to pass
With you across the flickering grass,
Mourns each inclined bough and leaf.

And I, with soul disquieted,
Shall find within the haunted spring
No peace, till your strange sorrowing
Is down the Tyrian distance fled.

Artemis

In the green and flowerless garden I have dreamt,
Lying beneath perennial moons apart,
Whose cypress-builded bowr's
And ivy-plighted myrtles none shall part;

In the funereal maze of larch and laurel,
Across white lawns, athwart the spectral
                                    mountains,
Seen through the sighing haze
Of all the high and moon-suspended fountains;

With feet enshaded by the fruitless green
Of summer trees that bear no summer blossom;
With wintry lusters laid
Upon the mounded marble of thy bosom,

Thou dost await, O mournful, enigmatic
Image of love-bewildered Artemis,
Whose tender lips too late,
Or all too soon, have sought the wounding kiss.

The City in the Desert

In a lost land, that only dreams have known,
Where flaming suns walk naked and alone;
Among horizons bright as molten brass,
And glowing heavens like furnaces of glass,
It rears, with dome and tower manifold,
Rich as a dawn of amarant and gold,
Or gorgeous as the Phoenix, born of fire,
And soaring from an opalescent pyre,
Sheer to the zenith. Like some anademe
Of Titan jewels turned to flame and dream,
The city crowns the far horizon-light,
Over the flowered meads of damassin.
A desert isle of madreperl! wherein
The thurifer and opal-fruited palm,
And heaven-thronging minarets becalm
The seas of azure wind.

NOTE: These lines were remembered out of a
dream, and are given verbatim.

The Melancholy Pool

Marked by that priesthood of the Night's misrule,
The shadow-cowled, imprecatory trees—
Cypress that guarded woodland secrecies
And graves that waited the delaying ghoul,
Nathless I neared the melancholy pool,
Chief care of all, but closelier sentinelled
By those whose roots were deepest in dead Eld.
Where the thwart-woven boughs were wet and
                                        cool,
As with a mist of poison, I drew near,
To mark the tired stars peer dimly down
Through riven branches from the height of space,
And shudder in those waters with quick fear,
Where in black deeps the pale moon seemed to
                                        drown—
A haggard girl, with dead, despairing face.

The Mirrors of Beauty

Beauty hath many mirrors: multifold
In ocean, or the foam, the gem, the dew,
Or well and rivulet, her eyes renew
With moon or sun their glories bright or cold,—
Whether in nights the ruby planets hold,
Or with the sombre light and icy hue
Of skies Decembral, or the autumn's blue,
Or dawn or evening of the vernal gold.

Often, upon the solitary sea,
She lieth, ere the wind shall gather breath—
One with the reflex of infinity.
In pools profounder for the twilight sky,
Her vision dwells, or in the poet's eye,
Or the black crystal of the eyes of Death.

Winter Moonlight

The silence of the silver night
Lies visibly upon the pines;
In marble flame the moon declines
Where spectral mountains dream in light.

And pale as with eternal sleep,
The enchanted valleys, far and strange,
Extend forever without change
Beneath the veiling splendours deep.

Carven of steel or fretted stone,
One stark and leafless autumn tree
With shadows made of ebony,
Leans on the moon-ward field alone.

To the Beloved

Green suns, and suns of garnet I have known—
Turning, with suns that mock the sapphire-gem,
The constellated moons that mirror them
To ever-changing opals. On the flown
Horizons I have followed, all alone,
To meadows of mirage the deserts hem,
And sought to break the ghostly, golden stem
Of roses of illusion, briefly blown
By evanescent waters. One by one,
The outward ways of wonder I have trod
Through alien lives ineffable. But none
Hath held the troublous marvel and surprise
That gleams and trembles in thy slightest nod,
Or sleeps between thy eyelids and thine eyes.

Love is not yours, love is not mine

Love is not yours, love is not mine:
It is the tranquil twilight heaven
Through which our pauseless feet are driven
Into the vast and desert noon.

Love is not mine, love is not yours:
It is a flying fire that passes,
Perishing on the blind morasses,
After the frail and perished moon

Requiescat

What was Love's worth,
Who lived with the roses?—
Love that is earth,
And with earth reposes!

What was Love's wonder?—
Scent of the flow'rs
After the thunder,
Thunder, and show'rs!

What were the breathless
Words that he said?—
Love that was deathless,
Love that is dead!

Echo hath taken
The song, and flown;
None shall awaken
Music and moan.

Buds and the flower,
All that Love found,
Last but an hour
Strewn on his mound.

Mirage

Deem ye the veiling vision will abide—
The marvel, and the glamour, and the dream,
Which lies in light upon the barren world?

The wings of Phoenix towering to the sun,
Nor opals, nor the morning foam, may hold
The hueful flame that as from faery moons
Is mirrored on the sand; where many a time,
From fields that hem with golden asphodel
A river like a dragon coiled in light,
Rise to the noon the hovering minarets
And soaring walls of cities Ilion-like,
Till the dim winds are hung with palaces
Of orient madreperl.

Forever lost—
Like sunset on a land of old romance,—
The splendour fails, and leaves the traveller
In endless deserts flaming to the day.

Inheritance

On all the sovereignty thine eyes obtain,
Thy grant of vision from the royal sun,
And all thine appanage of lordly dream,
The Dust, wherewith the worm is parcener,
Waits with perennial claim, nor will resign
Its right in thee: All glories and all gleams,
The seven splendours that inform the light,
And beauties immemorial as the moon,
Robing the barren world—all which thine eyes
Hold for inheritance, at length shall fill
The blindness and oblivion of the grave,
And leave it dark.

With dustiness and night
Upon thy mouth of starry proud desire,
With slumber for thy dreams, thou wilt repose,
Nor startle when the lazy, loitering Worm
Is slow to leave the tavern of thy brain.

Chant of Autumn

Like the voice of a golden star,
Heard from afar,
Perishing beauty calls
Out of the mist and rain;
Like the song of a silver wind,
When the night is blind,
Murmuring music falls,
Never to rise again.

Voice of the leaves that die,
Whisper and sigh
Of ruinous gardens waning
Rose by ungathered rose!
Dolour of pines immortal,
That guard the portal
Of a lonely mead retaining
Blossoms that no man knows!

Voices of love and the autumn sun—
In my heart ye are one!
Fairer the petals that fall,
Dearer the beauty that dies,
And the pyres of autumn burning,
Than a thousand springs returning.
O, perishing loves that call
In my heart and the hollow skies!

Autumnal

In all the pleasances where Love was lord,
Blossom the mournful immortelles alone;
The fallen roses crumble, and are blown,
A snow of red, about the barren sward.

The misty sun is grown a dimmer gold:
Only the leaves, the leaves forever seem
To tell and treasure, in a gorgeous dream,
The aureate fervour of the dawns of old.

Only for us remains the memory
Of sultry moons and summer suns that were;
And we have found, where fallen roses stir,
The immortelles that flower mournfully.

Echo of Memnon

I wandered ere the dream was done
Where over Nilus' nenuphars,
With all its ears of quivering stars,
The darkness listened for the sun.

Ere shadows were, ere night was gone,
I found the one whom suns had sought,
And waiting at his feet, methought
Had speech with Memnon in the dawn.

Sad as the last, lamenting star,
He sang, and clear as morning's gold:
Unto his voice I saw unfold
The hesitant, pale nenuphar.

But dolorous like the peal of dooms,
And proclamation of the night,
The waste returned that voice of light
With echo from its hollow tombs!

Twilight on the Snow

Before the hill's high altar bowed
The trees are Druids, weird and white,
Facing the vision of the light
With ancient lips to silence vowed.

No certain sound the woods aver,
Nor motion save of formless wings—
Filled with faint twilight flutterings,
With thronging gloom, and shadow-stir.

And hidden in a hollow dell,
Lie all the winds that magic trees
Have lulled with crystal wizardries,
And bound about with Merlin-spell.

Image

Calm as a long-forgotten marble god who smiles,
Colossal, in the grim serenity of stone,
Upon the broken pillars lying all alone,
Athwart the horizon's infinite and yellow miles;

Whom neither desert darkness nor the desert
                                        noon,
Nor dawns that render terrible the bare dead
                                        land,
Nor winds that wrap his mighty form in palls of
                                        sand,
Nor the Medusa of the dumb and stony moon,

Shall evermore dismay, nor lion, nor the lynx,
With silken-sheathèd claws, and eyes of golden
                                        glede;
Nor any griffin, from the gates of treasure freed
To roam the gulf, nor any wild and wandering
                                        sphinx:—

Even thus, amid the waste of all fair things that
                                        were,
Of high marmoreal dreams immense and
                                        overthrown,
I wait forever, and about my face is blown
The sand of crumbling cenotaph and sepulcher.

Nightmare

As though a thousand vampires, from the day
Fleeing unseen, oppressed that nightly deep,
The straitening and darkened skies of sleep
Closed on the dreamland dale in which I lay.

Eternal tensions numbed the wings of Time,
While through the unending narrow ways I sought
Awakening; up precipitous gloom I thought
To reach the dawn, far-pinnacled sublime.

Rejected at the closen gates of light
I turned, and down new dreams and shadows fled,
Where beetling Shapes of veiled, colossal dread
With Gothic wings enormous arched the night.

The Refuge of Beauty

From regions of the sun's half-dreamt decay,
All day the cruel rain strikes darkly down;
And from the night thy fatal stars shall frown—
Beauty, wilt thou abide this night and day?

Roofless, at portals dark and desperate,
Wilt thou a shelter unrefused implore,
And past the tomb's too-hospitable door,
Evade thy lover, in eluding Hate?

Alas, for what have I to offer thee?—
Chill halls of mind, dark rooms of memory
Where thou shalt dwell with woes and thoughts
                                                                        infirm;

This rumour-throngèd citadel of Sense,
Trembling before some nameless Imminence;
And fellow-guestship with the glutless Worm.

The Mummy

From out the light of many a mightier day,
From Pharaonic splendour, Memphian gloom,
And from the night aeonian of the tomb
They brought him forth, to meet the modern

ray,—

Upon his brow the unbroken seal of clay,
While gods have gone to a forgotten doom,
And desolation and the dust assume
Temple and cot immingling in decay.

From out the everlasting womb sublime
Of cyclopean death, within a land
Of tombs and cities rotting in the sun,
He is reborn to mock the might of time,
While kings have built against Oblivion
With walls and columns of the windy sand.

Forgetfulness

My life is less than any broken glass.
My long and weary love, thy lips unwon—
All, all is turned to mere oblivion,
With the grey flowers and the fallen grass
Of yesteryear. And on the winds that pass,
Thy music and thy memory are one;
For thy wan face, desired above the sun,
Only some languid echo saith Alas.

Love is no more, immemorably flown
As any leaf or petal.But to me,
The very fields are still, and strange, and lone:
The forest and the garden fail for breath,
Where the dumb heavens hold implacably
An autumn like the marble sleep of death.

The Chimaera

O, who will slay the last chimaera, Time?
Though Love and Death have many a cunning
                                          dart—
Despite of these, and close-wrought webs of Art,
And Slumber, with a slow Lethean lime—

Still, still, he lives; and though thy feet attain
The lunar peaks of ice and crystal, he,
Some night of agonized eternity
With brazen teeth shall gnaw thy fretted brain.

Gorged with the dust of thrones and fanes
                                       destroyed—
With lidless eyes like moons of adamant,
And vaulted mouth emportalling the void,

He crouches like a passive sphinx before
Some temple gate, or, grinning, moves to grant
Thine entrance at the monarch's golden door.

Satan Unrepentant

Lost from those archangelic thrones that star,
Fadeless and fixed, heaven's light of azure bliss;
Rejected of His splendour and depressed
Beyond the birth of the first sun, and lower
Than the last star's decline, I here endure,
Abased, majestic, fallen, beautiful,
And unregretful in the doubted dark,
Throneless, that greatens chaos-ward, albeit
From chanting stars that throng the nave of night
Lost echoes wander here, and of his praise,
With ringing moons for cymbals dinned afar,
And shouted from the flaming mouths of suns.
The shadows of impalpable blank deeps—
Deep upon deep accumulate—close down,
Around my head concentered, while above,
In the lit, loftier blue, star after star
Spins endless orbits betwixt me and heaven;
And at my feet mysterious Chaos breaks,
Abrupt, immeasurable. Round His throne
Now throbs the rhythmic resonance of suns,
Incessant, perfect, music infinite:
I, throneless, hear the discords of the dark,
And roar of ruin uncreate, than which
Some vast cacophony of dragons, heard
In wasted worlds, were purer melody.

The universe His tyranny constrains
Turns on: In old and consummated gulfs
The stars that wield His judgment wait at hand,
And in new deeps Apocalyptic suns

Prepare His coming: Lo, His mighty whim
To rear and mar, goes forth enormously
In nights and constellations! Darkness hears
Enragèd suns that bellow down the deep
God's ravenous and insatiable will;
And He is strong with change, and rideth forth
In whirlwind clothed, with thunders and with
                                                    doom,
To the red stars: God's throne is reared of change;
Its myriad and successive hands support
Like music His omnipotence, that fails
If mercy or if justice interrupt
The sequence of that tyranny, begun
Upon injustice, and doomed evermore
To stand thereby.

I, who with will not less
Than His, but lesser strength, opposed to Him
This unsubmissive brow and lifted mind,
He holds remote, in nullity and night
Doubtful between old Chaos and the deeps
Betrayed by Time to vassalage. Methinks
All tyrants fear whom they may not destroy,
And I, that am of essence one with His,
Though less in measure, He may not destroy,
And but withstands in gulfs of dark suspense,
A secret dread forever: For God knows
This quiet will irrevocably set
Against His own, and this mine old revolt
Yet stubborn, and confirmed eternally.
And with the hatred born of fear, and fed
Ever thereby, God hates me, and His gaze

Sees the bright menace of mine eyes afar,
Through midnight, and the innumerable blaze
Of servile suns: Lo, strong in tyranny,
The despot trembles that I stand opposed!
For fain am I to hush the anguished cries
Of Substance, broken on the racks of change,
Of Matter tortured into life; and God,
Knowing this, dreads evermore some huge
mishap—

That in the vigils of Omnipotence,
Once careless, I shall enter heaven, or He,
Himself, with weight of some unwonted act,
Thoughtless perturb His balanced tyranny,
To mine advance of watchful aspiration.

With rumored thunder and enormous groan—
(Burden of sound that heavens overborne
Let slip from deep to deep, even to this,
Where climb the huge cacophonies of Chaos)
God's universe moves on. Confirmed in pride,
In patient majesty serene and strong,
I wait the dreamt, inevitable hour,
Fulfilled of orbits ultimate, when God,
Whether through His mischance or mine own
deed,

Or rise of other and extremer Strength,
Shall vanish, and the lightened universe
No more remember Him than Silence does
An ancient thunder. I know not if these,
Mine all-indomitable eyes, shall see
A maimed and dwindled Godhead cast among
The stars of His creating, and beneath

The unnumbered rush of swift and shining feet,
Trodden into night; or mark the fiery breath
Of His infuriate suns blaze forth upon
And scorch that coarsened Essence; or His flame,
Drawn through the windy halls of nothingness,
A mightier comet, roar and redden down,
Portentous unto Chaos. I but wait,
In strong majestic patience equable,
That hour of consummation and of doom,
Of justice, and rebellion justified.

The Medusa of Despair

I may not mask forever with the grace
Of woven flow'rs thine eyes of staring stone:
Ere fatally I front thee, fully known
The guarded horror of thy haggard face,
Thy visage carven from the heart long dead
Of some white, frozen star; ere thou astound
My life to thine own likeness, and confound—
Depart, and curse more kindred things instead:

Triumphant, through what realms of elder doom
Where even the swart vans of Time are stunned,
Seek thou some fit, Cimmerian citadel,
And mighty cities, desolate, unsunned,
Whose walls of horrent and enormous gloom
Make sharp the horizon of the light of hell!

The Abyss Triumphant

The force of suns had waned beyond recall.
Chaos was re-established over all,
Where lifeless atoms through forgetful deeps
Fled unrelated, cold, immusical.

Above the tumult heaven alone endured;
Long since the bursting walls of hell had poured
Demon and damned to peace erstwhile denied,
Within the Abyss God's might had not immured.

(He could but thwart it with creative mace.)
And now it rose above the heavenly base,
Mordant at pillars rotten through and through
Of Matter's last, most firm abiding-place.

Bastion and minaret began to nod,
Till all the pile, unmindful of His rod,
Dissolved in thunder, and the void Abyss
Caught like a quicksand at the feet of God!

The Motes

I saw a universe to-day:
Through a disclosing bar of light
The motes were whirled in gleaming flight
That briefly dawned and sank away.

Each had its swift and tiny noon;
In orbit-streams I marked them flit,
Successively revealed and lit.
The sunlight paled and shifted soon.

Palms

Palms in the sunset of a languid summer land!
Sculpture of living green, on dreamy scarlet light
Dividing as a wall the twilight from the night!
How magically still and luminous they stand,

Inclining fretted leaves above some red lagoon—
Careless alike, in mystic and immense repose,
Of the flamingo-coloured, flying sun that goes,
Or the slow coming of the lion-coloured moon.

Laus Mortis

The imperishable phantoms, Love and Fame,
Nor Beauty, burning on the mist and mire
A fugitive uncapturable fire,
Nor God, that is a darkness and a name—
Not these, not these my choric dreams acclaim,
But Death, the last and ultimate desire,
Great Death I praise with litany and lyre,
And sombre pray'r implacably the same.

O, incommunicable hope that lies
Deep in despair, as tapers that illume
Some fearful fane's arcanic, sacred gloom!
O, solace of all weary hearts and wise!—
The dream which Satan hath for anodyne,
Which is to God a sweet and secret wine.

The Ghoul and the Seraph

Scene: A cemetery, by moonlight. The Ghoul emerges from the shade of a cypress, and sings.

THE SONG
Ho, ho, the Pest is on the wing!
Ha, ha, the sweet and crimson foam
Upon the lips of churl and king!
No worm but hath a feastful home:
Ha, ha, the Pest is on the wing!

Ho, ho, his kiss incarnadines
The brows of maiden, queen and whore!
The nun to him her cheek resigns;
Wan lips were never kissed before
His ancient kiss incarnadines.

Good cheer to thee, white worm of death!
The priest within the brothel dies,
The bawd hath sickened from his breath!
In grave half-dug the digger lies:
Good cheer to thee, white worm of death!

The Seraph appears from among the trees, half-walking, half-flying with wings whose iris the moonlight has rendered faint, and pauses abruptly at sight of the Ghoul.

THE SERAPH
What gardener in crudded fields of hell,
Or scullion of the Devil's house, art thou—
To whom the filth of Malebolge clings,
And reek of horrid refuse? Thou art gnurled
And black as any Kobold from the mines
Where demons delve for orichalch and steel
To forge the racks of Satan! On thy face,
Detestable and evil as might haunt
The last delirium of a dying hag,
Or necromancer's madness, fall thy locks,
Like sodden reeds that trail in Acheron
From shores of night and horror! And thy hands,
Like roots of cypresses uptorn in storm
That still retain their grisly provender,
Make the glad wine and manna of the skies
Turn to a qualmish sickness in my veins!

THE GHOUL
And who art thou?—Some white-faced fool of
God,
With wings that emulate the giddy bird,
And bloodless mouth forever filled with psalms
In lieu of honest victuals! Askest thou
My name? I am the Ghoul Necromalor:
In new-made graves I delve for sustenance,
As Man within his turnip-fields: I take
For table the uprooted slab, that bears
The words, "In Pace;" black and curdled blood
Of cadavers is all my cupless wine—
Slow-drunken, as the dainty vampire drinks
From pulses oped in never-ending sleep.

THE SERAPH

O! foulness born as of the ninefold curse
Of dragon-mouthed Apollyon, plumed with darts,
And armed with horns of incandescent bronze!
O, dark as Satan's nightmare, or the fruit
Of Belial's rape on hell's black hippogriff!
What knowest THOU of Paradise, where grow
The gardens of the manna-laden myrrh,
And lotos never known to Ulysses,
Whose fruit provides our long and sateless
                                    banquet?
Where boundless fields, unfurrowed and unsown,
Supply for God's own appanage their foison
Of amber-hearted grain, and sesame
Sweeter than nard the Persian air compounds
With frankincense from isles of India?
Where flame-leaved forests infinitely teem
With palms of tremulous opal, from whose top
Ambrosial honeys fall forevermore
In rains of nacred light! Where rise and rise
Terrace on hyacinthine terrace, hills
Hung with the grapes that drip cerulean wine,
One draught whereof dissolves eternity
In bliss oblivious and supernal dream!

THE GHOUL

To all, the meat their bellies most commend,
To all, the according wine: For me, I wot,
The cates whereof thou braggest were as wind
In halls where men had feasted yesterday,
Or furbished bones the full hyena leaves:
Tiger and pig have their apportioned glut,

Nor lacks the shark his provender; the bird
Is nourished with the worm of charnels; man,
Or the grey wolf, will slay and eat the bird,
Till wolf and man be carrion for the worm.
What wouldst thou? As the elfin lily does,
Or as the Paphian myrtle, pink with love,
I draw me from the unreluctant dead
The rightful meat my belly's law demands.
Eaters of death are all: Life shall not live,
Save that its food be death; No atomy
In any star, or heaven's remotest moon,
But hath a billion billion times been made
The food of insatiable life, and food
Of death insatiate: For all is change—
Change, that hath wrought the chancre and the
rose,
And wrought the star, and wrought the sapphire-
stone,
And lit great altars, and the eyes of lions—
Change, that hath made the very gods from slime
Drawn from the pits of Python, and will fling
Gods and their builded heavens back again
To slime. The fruits of archangelic light
Thou braggest of, and grapes of azure wine,
Have been the dung of dragons, and the blood
Of toads in Phlegethon; each particle
That is their splendour, clomb in separate ways,
Through suns, and worlds, and cycles infinite—
Through burning brume of systems unbegun,
Or manes of long-haired comets, that have lashed
The night of space to fury and to fire;
And in the core of cold and lightless stars,
And in immalleable metals deep.

Each atomy hath slept, or known the slime
Of Cyclopean oceans turned to air
Before the suns of Ophinchus rose;
And they have known the interstellar night,
And they have lain at root of sightless flowr's
In worlds without a sun, or at the heart
Of monstrous-eyed and panting flow'rs of flesh,
Or aeon-blooming amaranths of stone:
And they have ministered within the brains
Of sages and magicians, and have served
To swell the pulse of kings or conquerors,
And have been privy to the hearts of queens.

The Ghoul turns his back on the Seraph, and
moves away singing.

THE SONG
O condor, keep thy mountain-ways,
Above the long Andean lands!
Gier-eagle, guard the eastern sands
Where the forsaken camel strays!
Beetle and worm and I will ward
The feastful graves of lout and lord.

O, warm and bright the blood that lies
Upon the wounded lion's trail!
Hyena, laugh, and jackal, wail
And ring him round, who turns and dies!
Beetle and worm and I will ward
The feastful graves of lout and lord.

Raven and kestrel, kite and crow,
The swart patrol of northern lands,
Gather your noisy, bickering bands—
The reindeer bleeds upon the snow!
Beetle and worm and I will ward
The feastful graves of lout and lord.

Arms of a wanton girl are good,
Or hands of harp-player and knight!
Breasts of the nun be sweet and white,
Sweet is the festive friar's blood!
Beetle and worm and I will ward
The feastful graves of lout and lord.

At Sunrise

The moon declines in lonely gold
Among the stars of ashen-grey—
Veiling the pallors of decay
With clouds and glories, fold on fold.

Within a crystal interlude,
Stillness and twilight rest awhile
Ere the bright snows, illumined, smile,
From peaks where sullen purples brood;

And from the low Favonian bourn,
A light wind blows so dulcetly
It seems the futile silver sigh
Breathed by the lingering moon forlorn.

The Land of Evil Stars

'Neath blue days, and gold, and green,
Blooms the glorious land serene,—
Flaming shields of dawns between;
And the rapt white flowers suffice
To illume
With their bright eyes
Fluctuant ecstatic gloom
'Twixt the fallen emerald sun,
And the unrisen azure one.

But the season of the night
Comes in all the suns' despite;
And, ah, gorgeous then their sorrows,
At departure into morrows
Of far, other lands forgot—
Until now remembered not,
For the lovelier flow'rs of this,
And each lake's pure lucency;
And recalled regretfully,
Regretfully, for leaving THIS.

In the star-possessèd night
The land knows another light—
All the small and evil rays
Of the sorcerous orbs ablaze
With ecstatical, intense
Hate and still malevolence—

Dwelling on the fields below
From the ascendancy of even,
Till the suns, re-entering heaven,
Glorify with triple glow
The dim flowers smitten low.

Ah, not cold, or kind, as ours,
The stars of those remotest hours!
Peace and pallor of the flow'rs
They have fevered, they have marred,
With the poison of their light,
With distillèd bale and blight
Of a red, accursed regard:
All the toil of sunlight hours
They undo
With their wild eyes—
Eldritch and ecstatic eyes,
Stooping timeward from the skies,
Burning redly in the dew.

The Harlot of the World

O Life, thou harlot who beguilest all!
Beautiful in thy house, the gorgeous world,
Abidest thou, where Powers pinion-furled
And flying Splendours follow to thy call.

Innumerous like the stars or like the dust,
Nations and monarchs were thy thralls of yore:
Unto the grave's old womb forevermore
Hast thou betrayed the passion and the lust.

Fair as the moon of summer is thy face,
And mystical with cloudiness of hair.
Only an eye, subornless by delight,

Shall find within thy phosphorescent gaze
Those caverns of corruption and despair,
Where the Worm toileth in the charnel night.

The Hope of the Infinite

My hope is in the unharvestable deep,
That shows with eve the treasure of the stars
To mournful kings behind their palace-bars,
And wanderers outworn, and boys who weep
A shattered bauble—or above the sleep
Of headsmen, and of men condemned to die,
Pours out the moon's white mercy from on high,
Or hides with clement gloom the hours that creep
Like death-worms to the grave. And I have ta'en
From storming seas by sunset glorified,
Or from the dawn of ashen wastes and wide,
Some light re-gathered from the lamps that wane,
And promise of a translunary Spain,
Where loves forgone and forfeit dreams abide.

Love Malevolent

I fain would love thee, but thy lips are fed
With poison-honey, hivèd in a skull;
They seem like scarlet poppies, beautiful
For delving roots, deep-clenchèd in the dead.

Thine eyes are coloured like the nightshade-flow'r.
Blent in the opiate perfume of thy breath
Are dreams, and purple sleep, and scented death
For him that is thy lover for an hour.

Mandragora, within the graveyard grown,
Hath given thee its carnal root to eat,
And vipers, born and nurstled in a tomb,

From fawning mouths drip venom at thy feet;
Yet from thy lethal lips and thine alone,
Love would I drink, as dew from poison-bloom.

Memnon at Midnight

Methought upon the tomb-encumbered shore
I stood, of Egypt's lone, monarchal stream,
And saw immortal Memnon, throned supreme
In gloom as of that Memphian night of yore:
Fold upon fold purpureal he wore,
Beneath the star-borne canopy extreme—
Carven of silence and colossal dream,
Where waters flowed like sleep forevermore.

Lo, in the darkness, thick with dust of years,
How many a ghostly god around his throne,
With thronging winds that were forgotten Fames,
Stood, ere the dawn restore to ancient ears
The long-withholden thunder of their names,
And music stilled to monumental stone.

Eidolon

Chryselephantine, clear as carven flame,
Before my gaze, thy soul's eidolon stands,
As on the threshold of the frozen lands
A frozen sun forevermore the same.

All passion that the passive marbles make
Imperishable in their shining sleep,
Is thine; and all the wan despairs that weep
With tears of ice and crystal, cannot break

The heart, which, like a ruby white and rare,
In thy deep breast impenetrably gleams.
More beautiful than any sphynx, and fair

As Aphrodite dead, thine image seems—
Guarding forever, in its golden eyes,
The treasure of intagliate memories.

The Kingdom of Shadows

A crownless king who reigns alone,
I live within this ashen land,
Where winds rebuild from wandering sand
My columns and my crumbled throne.

My sway is on the men that were,
And wan sweet women, dear and dead;
Beside a marble queen, my bed
Is made within the sepulchre.

In gardens desolate to the sun,
Faring alone, I sigh to find
The dusty closes, dim and blind,
Where winter and the spring are one.

My shadowy visage, grey with grief,
In sunken waters walled with sand,
I see,—where all mine ancient land
Lies yellow like an autumn leaf.

My silver lutes of subtle string
Are rust,—but on the grievous breeze,
I hear what sobbing memories.
And muted sorrows murmuring!

Across the broken monuments,
Memorial of the dreams of old,
The sunset flings a ghostly gold
To mock mine ancient affluence.

About the tombs of stone and brass
The silver lights of evening flee;
And slowly now, and solemnly,
I see the pomp of shadows pass.
Often, beneath some fervid moon,
With splendid spells I vainly strive
Dead loves imperial to revive,
And speak a heart-remembered rune:—

But, ah, the lovely phantoms fail,
The faces fade to mist and light,
The vermeil lips of my delight
Are dim, the eyes are ashen-pale.
A crownless king who reigns alone,
I live within this ashen land,
Where winds rebuild from wandering sand
My columns and my crumbled throne.

Sepulture

Deep in my heart, as in the hollow stone
And silence of some olden sepulchre,
Thy silver beauty lies, and shall not stir—
Forgotten, incorruptible, alone:
Though altars darken, and a wind be blown
From starless seas on beacon-fires that were—
Within thy tomb, with oils of balm and myrrh,
Forever burn the onyx lamps unknown.

And though the bleak, Novembral gardens yield
Rose-dust and ivy-leaf, nor any flow'r
Be found through vermeil forest or wan field—
Still, still the asphodel and lotos lie
Around thy bed, and hour by silent hour,
Exhale immortal fragrance like a sigh.

A Precept

With words of ivory,
Of bronze, of ebony,
Of alabaster, marble, steel, and gold,
The beauty of the visible is told.

But how with these express
The unseen Loveliness—
Splendour and light, and harmony, and sound,
The heart hath felt, the sense hath never found?

No shining words of stone—
Shadow and cloud alone—
These shall the poet seek eternally,
Whose lines would carve the mask of Mystery.

Requiescat in Peace

White iris on thy bier,
With the white rose, we strew,
And lotus pale or blue
As moonlight on the orient mountain-snows.

Slumber, as they that sleep
In the slow sands unknown,
Or under seas that zone
With lulling foam the sealed, extremer lands.

Slumber, with songless birds
That sang, and sang to death,
Giving their gladder breath
To lonely winds in one melodious pang.

Sleep, with the golden queens
Of planets long forgot,
Whose fire-soft lips are not
Recalled by any sorcery of song.

Sleep, with the flowers that were,
And any leaf that fell
On field or flowerless dell
In autumns lost of memory and grief.

Pass, with the music flown
From ivory lyre, and lute
Of mellow string left mute
In cities desolate ere the dream of Tyre.

Pass, with the clouds that sank
In sunset turned to grey
On some Edenic day
For which the exiled years have ever yearned.

White iris on thy bier,
With the white rose, we strew,
And lotus pale or blue
As moonlight on the orient mountain-snows.

Alexandrines

Knowing the weariness of dreams, and days, and
nights,
    The great and grievous vanity of joy and pain;
    Frail loves that pass, where languors infinite
                remain;
    Fervours, and long despairs, and desperate, brief
                delights;

Knowing how in the witless brains of them that
                were,
    The drowsy, wiving worm hath prospered and
                hath died;
    Knowing that, evermore, by moon and sun abide
    The standing glooms made stagnant in the
                sepulchre;

Knowing the vacillant leaves that tremble, flame,
                and fall,
    The sweetly wasting rose, the dawns and stars
                that wane—
    Knowing these things, the desolate heart and soul
                are fain
Of the one perfect sleep which filleth, foldeth all.

Ashes of Sunset

Who fares to find the sunset ere it fly,
Turning to light and fire the further west,
Shall have the veils of twilight for his quest,
And all the falling of an ashen sky.

On lands he shall not know, the splendour lies—
A pharos on some alienated shore,
In foam and purple lost forevermore,
Where dreams are kindled in remoter eyes.

November Twilight

November's winy sunset leaves,
Deep in the silver heavens far,
One ruby-hearted star
That lit the summer's moon-forsaken eves.

Under its ray, remote, alone,
Ascends upon the ashen gloom
The ghostly, faint perfume
From autumn's grey, forgotten roses flown.

Quest

All beneath a wintering sky
Follow the wastrel butterfly;
With vermilion leaf or bronze—
Tatters of gorgeous gonfalons—
With the winds that always hold
Echo of clarions lost and old,—
We must hasten, hasten on
Tow'rd the azure world withdrawn,
We must wander, wander so
Where the ruining roses go;
Where the poplar's pallid leaves
Drift among the gathered sheaves
In that harvest none shall glean;
Where the twisted willows lean
In their strange, tormented woe,
Seeing, on the streamlet's flow
Half their fragile leaves depart;
Where the secret pines at heart,
High, funereal, vespertine,
Guard eternal sorrows green:—
We shall follow, we shall find,
Haply, ere the light is blind,
The moulded place where Beauty lay,
Moon-beheld until the day,
In the woven windlestrae;
Or the pool of tourmaline,
Rimmed with golden reeds, that was
In the dawn a tiring-glass
For her undelaying mien.

Ever wander, wander so,
Where the ruining roses go;
All beneath a wintering sky,
Follow the wastrel butterfly.

Beauty Implacable

White Beauty, bending from a throne sublime,
Hath claimed my lips with kisses keen as snow:
Now through my harp the tremors come and go
Of things not stirred with urgencies of Time.
Now from the lunar mountains, old and lone,
In dream I watch the neighboring world remote;
Or on the dim Uranian waters float
After a star-like sun from zone to zone.

Lo! in her praise, the stern, the fearful one,
Whose love is as the light of snows afar,
Whose ways are difficult, what word shall be?
I, desolate with Beauty, and undone,
Say Death is not so strong to change or mar,
And Love and Life not so desired as she.

Desire of Vastness

Supreme with night, what high mysteriarch—
The undreamt-of god beyond the trinal noon
Of elder suns empyreal—past the moon
Circling some wild world outmost in the dark—
Lays on me this unfathomed wish to hark
What central sea with plume-plucked midnight
                                        strewn,
Plangent to what enormous plenilune
That lifts in silence, hinderless and stark?

The brazen comprehension of the waste,
The waste inclusion of the brazen sky—
These I desire, and all things wide and deep;
And, lifted past the level years, would taste
The cup of an Olympian ecstasy,
Titanic dream, and Cyclopean sleep.

Anticipation

The thought of death to me
Is like a well of waters, deep and dim—
Cool-gleaming, hushed, and hidden gratefully
Among the palms asleep
At silver evening on the desert's rim.

Or as a couch of stone,
Whereon by moonlight, in a marble room,
Some fevered king reposes all alone—
So is the hope of sleep,
The inalienable surety of the tomb.

Flamingoes

On skies of tropic evening, broad and beryl-green,
Above a tranquil sea of molten malachite,
With flare of scarlet wings, in long and level flight,
The soundless, fleet flamingoes pass to isles
                                             unseen.

They pass and disappear, where darkening palms
                                             indent
The horizon, underneath some high and tawny
                                             star—
Lost in the sunset gulfs of glowing cinnabar,
Where sinks the painted moon, with prows of
                                             orpiment.

A Psalm to the Best Beloved

Thou comfortest me with the manna of thy love,
And the kisses of thy mouth are wine and
                                    sustenance;
Thy lips are grateful as fruit
In lonely orchards by the wayside of a ruinous
                                    land;
They are sweet as the purple grapes
On parching hills that confront the autumnal
                                    desert,
Or apples that the mad simoon hath spared
In a garden with walls of syenite.
Thy loosened hair is a veil
For the weariness of mine eyes and eyelids,
Which have known the redoubled sun
In a desert valley with slopes of the dust of white
                                    marble,
And have gazed on the mounded salt
In the marshes of a lake of dead waters.
Thy body is a secret Eden
Fed with lethean springs,
And the touch of thy flesh is like to the savour of
                                    lotos.
In thy hair is a perfume of ecstasy,
And a perfume of sleep,
Between thy thighs is a valley of delight,
And between thy breasts is a valley of peace.

A Vision of Lucifer

I saw a shape with human form and face,
If such in apotheosis might stand:
Deep in the shadows of a desolate land
His burning feet obtained colossal base,
And spheral on the lonely arc of space,
His head, a menace unto heavens unspanned,
Arose with towered eyes that might command
The sunless, blank horizon of that place

And straight I knew him for the mystic one
That is the brother, born of human dream,
Of man rebellious at an unknown rod;
The mind's ideal, and the spirit's sun;
A column of clear flame in lands extreme,
Set opposite the darkness that is God.

The Witch in the Graveyard

Scene: A forsaken graveyard, by moonlight. Enter
two witches.

FIRST WITCH:
Sit, sister, now that haggish Hecate
Appropriate and ghastly favour sheds,
And with wild light forwards our enterprise;
And watch the weighted eyelids of each grave
As never mother watched her babe, to mark,
At zenith of the necromantic moon
The stir of that disquiet, when the dead,
From suckling nightmares of the charnel dark
Or long insomnia on a mouldy couch,
Impelled like wan somnambulists, arise—
Constrained to emerge and walk, or seated each
On his own tombstone, shrouded council hold,
Or commerce with the sooty wings of Hell.
All omens of this influential hour
When all dark powers, thronging to the dark,
Promote enchantry with their wavèd wings,
And brim the wind with potency malign—
A dew of dread to aid our cauldron—these
Observe thou closely, while I seek afield
All requisite swart herbs of venefice,
And evil roots unto our usance ripe.

(The first witch departs, leaving the other among the tombs, and returns after a time, in the course of her search.)

FIRST WITCH:
Sister, what seest or what hearest thou?

SECOND WITCH:
I see
The moonlight, and the slowly moving gleam
That westers hour by hour on tomb and stone;
And shrivelled lilies, tossed i' the winter's breath,
With their attenuate shadows, as might dance
Phantom with flaffing phantom; at my side,
The white and shuddering grasses of the grave,
With nettles, and the parching fumitory,
Whose leaves, root-trellised on the bones of death,
Will rasp and bristle to the lightest wind.

(The first witch moves on, and approaches again, after a long interval.)

FIRST WITCH:
Sister, what seest or what hearest thou?

SECOND WITCH:
I see
The mound-stretched gossamers, cradles to the
dew;
Moon-wefted briers, and the cypress-trees
With shadow swathed, or cerements of the moon;
And corpse-lights borne from aisle to secret aisle
Within the footless forest.

Now I hear
The lich-owl, shrieking lethal prophecy;
And whimpering winds, the children of the air,
Lost in the glades of mystery and gloom.

(The first witch disappears and passes again
shortly.)

FIRST WITCH:
Sister, what seest or what hearest thou?

SECOND WITCH:
I see
The ghost-white owl, with huge sulphureous eyes,
That veers in prone, unwhispered flight, and hear
The small shriek of the moon-adventuring mole,
Gripped in mid-graveyard. And I see
Where some wild shadow shakes, though the pale
wind
Of moonlight stirs far offand hear
Curst mandragores that gibber to the moon,
Though no man treads anigh.

(After an interval)

Some predal hand doth halt the wandering air;
Now dies the throttled wind with rattling breath,
And round about a breathing Silence prowls.

(After another interval)

I hear the cheeping of the bat-lipped ghouls,
Aroused beneath the vaulted cypresses
Far-off; and lipless muttering of tombs,
With clash of bones bestirred in ancient charnels
Beneath their shroud of unclean light that crawls.
Earth shudders, and rank odours 'gin to rise
From tombs a-crack; and shaken out all at once
From mid-air, and directly neath the moon,
Meseems what hanging wing divides the light,
Like a black film of gloom, or thickest shadow;
But on the tombs there is no shadow!

FIRST WITCH:
Enough! 'Twill be a prosperous night, methinks,
For commerce of the demons with the dead;
And for us, too, when every omen's good,
And fraught with, promise of a potent brew.

Poems in Prose

The Traveller

"Stranger, where goest thou, in the sad raiment of a pilgrim, with shattered sandals retaining the dust and mire of so many devious ways! With thy brow that alien suns have darkened, and thy hair made white from the cold rime of alien moons? Wanderest thou in search of the cities greater than Rome, with walls of opal and crystal, and fanes more white than the summer clouds, or the foam of hyperboreal seas? Or farest thou to the lands unpeopled and unexplored, to the sunless deserts lit by the baleful and calamitous beacons of volcanoes? Or seekest thou an extremer shore, where the red and monstrous lilies are like a royal pageant, pausing with innumerable flambeaux held aloft on the verge of the waveless waters?"

"Nay, it is none of these that I seek, but forevermore I seek the city and the land of my former home: In the quest thereof I have wandered from the first immemorial years of my youth till now, and have mingled the dust of many realms, of many highways, in my garments' hem. I have seen the cities greater than Rome, and the fanes more white than the clouds of summer; the lands unpeopled and unexplored, and the land that is thronged by the red and monstrous lilies. Even the far, aerial walls of the cities of mirage, and the saffron meadows of sunset I

have seen, but nevermore the city and land of my
former home."

"Where lieth the land of thine home? and by what
name shall we know it, and distinguish the rumour
thereof, among the rumours of many lands?"

"Alas! I know not where it lieth; nor in the broad,
black scrolls of geographers, and the charts of old
seamen who have sailed to the marge of the seventh
sea, is the place thereof recorded. And its name I have
never learned, howbeit I have learned the name of
empires lying beneath stars to us invisible. In many
languages have I spoken, in barbarous tongues
unknown to Babel; and I have heard the speech of
many men, even of them that inhabit the strange isles
of the sea of fire and the sea of snow. Thunder, and
lutes, and battle-drums, the fine unceasing
querulousness of gnats, and the stupendous moaning
of the simoon; lyres of ebony, damascened with
crystal, bells of malachite with golden clappers; the
song of exotic birds that sigh like women or sob like
fountains; whispers and shoutings of fire, the
multitudinous mutter of cities asleep, the manifold
tumult of cities at dawn, and the slow and weary
murmur of desert-wandering streams—all, all have I
heard, but never, in any place, from any tongue, a
sound or syllable that resembled in the least the name
I would learn."

The Flower-Devil

In a basin of porphyry, at the summit of a pillar of serpentine, the thing has existed from primeval time, in the garden of the kings that rule an equatorial realm of the planet Saturn. With black foliage, fine and intricate as the web of some enormous spider; with petals of livid rose, and purple like the purple of putrefying flesh; and a stem rising like a swart and hairy wrist from a bulb so old, so encrusted with the growth of centuries that it resembles an urn of stone, the monstrous flower holds dominion over all the garden. In this flower, from the years of the oldest legend, an evil demon has dwelt—a demon whose name and whose nativity are known to the superior magicians and mysteriarchs of the kingdom, but to none other. Over the half-animate flowers, the ophidian orchids that coil and sting, the bat-like lilies that open their ribbèd petals by night, and fasten with tiny yellow teeth on the bodies of sleeping dragonflies; the carnivorous cacti that yawn with green lips beneath their beards of poisonous yellow prickles; the plants that palpitate like hearts, the blossoms that pant with a breath of venomous perfume—over all these, the Flower-Devil is supreme, in its malign immortality, and evil, perverse intelligence—inciting them to strange maleficence, fantastic mischief, even to acts of rebellion against the gardeners, who proceed about their duties with wariness and trepidation, since more than one of them has been bitten, even unto death, by some vicious and venefic flower. In places, the garden has run wild from lack of care on the part of the fearful gardeners, and has become a monstrous tangle of serpentine creepers, and hydra-headed plants, convolved and inter-writhing in lethal hate or venomous love, and horrible as a rout of wrangling vipers and pythons.

And, like his innumerable ancestors before him, the king dares not destroy the Flower, for fear that the devil, driven from its habitation, might seek a new home, and enter into the brain or body of one of the king's subjects—or even the heart of his fairest and gentlest, and most beloved queen!

Images

TEARS

Thy tears are not as mine: Thou weepest as a green fountain among palms and roses, with lightly falling drops that bedew the flowery turf. My tears are like a rain of marah in the desert, leaving a bitter pool whose waters are fire and poison.

THE SECRET ROSE

My soul hath dreamt of a rose, whose marvellous and secret flower, fraught with an unimaginable perfume, hath never grown in any garden. Only in valleys of the shifting cloud, only among the palms and fountains of a land of mirage, only in isles beyond the seas of sunset, it blooms for a moment, and is gone. But ever the ghost of its fragrance haunts the hall of slumber; and the women whom I meet in dreams wear always its blossom for coronal.

THE WIND AND THE GARDEN

To thee my love is something strange and fantastical, and far away, like the vast and desolate sighing of the desert wind to one who dwells in a garden of palm and rose and lotus, filled by no louder sound than the mellow lisp of a breeze of perfume, or the sigh of silvering fountains.

OFFERINGS

Before thee, O goddess of my dreams, idol of my desires, I have burnt amber and myrrh, frankincense, and all the strange and rich perfumes of lands a thousand leagues beyond Araby or Taprobane. Strange and rich offerings have I brought thee, the gems of unknown regions, and the spoil of cities remoter than Caydon or Samarkand. But these delight thee not, only the simple-scented flowers of spring, and the diamonds and opals of dew, strung on the threads of the spider.

A CORONAL

The pale and flowerless poppies of Proserpine, the cold, blind lotus of Lethe, and the strange, white sea-blooms that grow from the lips of drowned men in the blue darkness of the nether sea,—these have I woven as a coronal for my dead love.

The Black Lake

In a land where weirdness and mystery had strongly leagued themselves with eternal desolation, the lake was out-poured at an undiscoverable date of elder aeons, to fill some fathomless gulf far down amid the shadows of snowless, volcanic mountains. No eye, not even the sun's, when he stared vertically upon it for a few hours at midday, seemed able to divine its depths of sullen blackness and unrippled silence. It was for this reason that I found a so singular pleasure in frequently contemplating the strange lake. Sitting for I knew not how long on its bleak basaltic shores, where grew but a few fleshly red orchids, bent above the waters like open and thirsty mouths, I would peer with countless fantastic conjectures and shadowy imaginings, into the alluring mystery of its unknown and inexplorable gulf.

It was at an hour of morning before the sun had surmounted the rough and broken rim of the summits, when I first came, and clomb down through the shadows which filled like some subtler fluid the volcanic basin. Seen at the bottom of that stirless tincture of air and twilight, the lake seemed as dregs of darkness.

Peering for the first time, after the deep and difficult descent, into the so dull and leaden waters, I was at length aware of certain small and scattered gleams of silver, apparently far beneath the surface.

And fancying them the metal in some mysterious ledge, or the glints of long-sunken treasure, I bent closer in my eagerness, and finally perceived that what I saw was but the reflection of the stars, which, tho the day was full upon the mountains and the lands without, were yet visible in the depth and darkness of that enshadowed place.

Remoteness

There are days when all the beauty of the world is dim and strange; when the sunlight about me seems to fall on a land remoter than the poles of the moon. The roses in the garden surprise me, like the monstrous orchids of unknown colour, blossoming in planets beyond Aldebaran. And I am startled by the yellow and purple leaves of October, as if the veil of some tremendous and awful mystery were half-withdrawn for a moment. In such hours as these, O heart of my heart, I fear to touch thee, I avoid thy caresses, dreading that thou wilt vanish as a dream at dawn; or that I shall find thee a phantom, the spectre of one who died and was forgotten many thousand years ago, in a far-off land on which the sun no longer shines.

Vignettes

BEYOND THE MOUNTAINS

Surely, beyond the mountains there is peace—beyond the mountains that lie so blue and still at the world's extreme. Such ancient calm, such infinite quietude is upon them, that surely, no toiling cities, no sea whose foam a ship has ever cloven, can lie beyond, but valleys of azure silence, where amaranthine flowers sleep and dream, untroubled of any wind, by the hyalescense of tranquilly flowing streams unbroken as the surface of a mirror.

THE BROKEN LUTE

Because you are silent to my lyric prayers, deaf to the melodies I have made from the sighs and murmurs of a wounded love, I have broken my golden lute, and cast it away, tarnished and unstrung, among the red leaves and faded roses of the September garden. Silence, the silver dust of lilies, the mournful muted wind of autumn, and the fitfully drifting leaves, have claimed it for their own. Seeing it there, as you pass on your queenly way amid the crumbling roses, will you not echo in your heart one sigh of the many sighs, which, as a music for your pleasure, were breathed from its chords, during the summer's half-forgotten days?

NOSTALGIA OF THE UNKNOWN

The nostalgia of things unknown, of lands forgotten or unfound, is upon me at times. Often I long for the gleam of yellow suns upon terraces of translucent azure marble, mocking the windless waters of lakes unfathomably calm; for lost, legendary palaces of serpentine, silver and ebony, whose columns are green stalactites; for the pillars of fallen temples, standing in the vast purpureal sunset of a land of lost and marvellous romance. I sigh for the dark-green depths of cedar forests, through whose fantastically woven boughs, one sees at intervals an unknown tropic ocean, like gleams of blue diamond; for isles of palm and coral, that fret an amber morning, somewhere beyond Cathay or Taprobana; for the strange and hidden cities of the desert, with burning brazen domes and slender pinnacles of gold and copper, that pierce a heaven of heated lazuli.

GREY SORROW

Ofttimes, in the golden, sad, November days, I meet among the dead roses of the garden the ghost of an old sorrow—a sorrow grey and dim as the mist of autumn—as a wandering mist that was once a rain of tears. There, through the long decline of afternoon, I walk among the roses with the ghost of my sorrow, whose half-forgotten, half-invisible form becomes dimmer and more indistinct, till I know its face no longer from the twilight, nor its voice from the vesper wind.

THE HAIR OF CIRCE

I am afraid of thy hair: Lustrous, heavily curled, it suggests the coils of a golden snake; and half the fascination of thy painted lips, of thy still and purple-lidded eyes, is due to the fear that it may awake beneath my caresses.

THE EYES OF CIRCE

Thine eyes are green and still as the lakes of the desert. They awake in me the thirst for strange and bitter mysteries, the desire of secrets that are deadly and sterile.

The Statue of Silence

I saw a statue, carven I knew not from what substance, nor with what form or feature, because of the manifold drapery of black which fell about it as a veil or a pall. Turning to Psyche, who was with me, I said, "O thou who knowest by name and form the eidola of all things, pray tell me what thing is this." And she answered, "The name of it is Silence, but neither god nor man nor demon knoweth the form thereof, nor its entity. The seraphim pause often before it, waiting the day when the shape shall be unveiled; and the gods and demons of the universe are mute in its presence, half-hoping, half-fearing the time when these lips shall speak, and deliver forth one dreameth not what, of oracle, or query or judgment, or doom."

A Dream of Lethe

In the quest of her whom I had lost, I came at length to the shores of Lethe, under the vault of an immense, empty, ebon sky, from which all the stars had vanished one by one. Proceeding I knew not whence, a pale, elusive light as of the waning moon, or the phantasmal phosphorescence of a dead sun, lay dimly and without lustre on the sable stream, and on the black, flowerless meadows. By this light, I saw many wandering souls of men and women, who came, hesitantly or in haste, to drink of the slow unmurmuring waters. But among all these, there were none who departed in haste, and many who stayed to watch, with unseeing eyes, the calm and waveless movement of the stream. At length in the lily-tall and gracile form, and the still, uplifted face of a woman who stood apart from the rest, I saw the one whom I had sought; and, hastening to her side, with a heart wherein old memories sang like a nest of nightingales, was fain to take her by the hand. But in the pale, immutable eyes, and wan, unmoving lips that were raised to mine, I saw no light of memory, nor any tremor of recognition. And knowing now that she had forgotten, I turned away despairingly, and finding the river at my side, was suddenly aware of my ancient thirst for its waters, a thirst I had once thought to satisfy at many diverse springs, but in vain. Stooping hastily, I drank, and rising again, perceived that the light had died or disappeared, and that all the land was like the land of a dreamless slumber, wherein I could no longer distinguish the faces of my companions. Nor was I able to remember any longer why I had wished to drink of the waters of oblivion.

The Princess Almeena

From her balcony of pearl the princess Almeena, clad in a gown of irisated silk, with her long and sable locks unbound, gazes toward the sunset-flooded sea beyond a terrace of green marble that peacocks guard. Below, in the tinted light, fantastic trees whose boles are serpentine, train a fine and hair-like foliage, mingling with the moon-shaped leaves of enormous lilies. Rainbow-coloured reeds cluster about the pools and fountains of black water, that are rimmed with carven malachite. But these the princess does not heed, but gazes upon the far-off seas, where the golden ichors of the sun have gathered in a vast lake overflowing the horizon. Ere long, a wind from the west, from islands where palm trees blossom above the purple foam, brings in its breath the odour of unknown flowers to mingle with the balms of the garden, and the sweet suspiration of the princess—the princess who dreams, listening to the wind, that her lover, the captain of the emperor's most redoubtable trireme of war, sailing the sky-blue seas beyond the horizon and the sunset, has remembered her wild and royal loveliness, and has breathed in his heart a secret sigh.

The Caravan

My dreams are like a caravan that departed long ago, with tumult of intrepid banners and spears, and the clamour of bugles and brave adventurous songs, to seek the horizons of perilous untried barbaric lands, and kingdoms immense and vaguely rumoured, with cities beautiful and opulent as the cities of paradise, and deep Edenic vales of palm and cinnamon and myrrh, lying beneath skies of primeval azure silence. For traffic in the realms of mystery and wonder, in the marts of scarce-imaginable cities and metropoli a million leagues away, on the last horizon of romance, my dreams departed, as a caravan with its laden camels. Since then, the years are many, the days have flown as the flocks of southering swallows; unnumbered moons have multiplied in fugitive silver, uncounted suns in irretainable gold. But, alas, my dreams have not returned. Have the swirling sands engulfed them, on a noon of storm when the desert rose like a sea, and rolled its tawny billows on the walled gardens of the green and fragrant lands? Or perished they, devoured by the crimson demons of thirst, and the ghouls and vultures? Or live they still, as captives in alien dungeons not to be ascertained, or held by a wizard spell in palaces demon-built, and cities baroque and splendid as the cities in a tale from the Thousand and One Nights?

Ennui

In the alcove whose curtains are cloth-of-gold, and whose pillars are fluted sapphire, reclines the emperor Chan, on his couch of ebony set with opals and rubies, and cushioned with the furs of unknown and gorgeous beasts. With implacable and weary gaze, from beneath unmoving lids that seem carven of purple-veined onyx, he stares at the crystal windows, giving upon the infinite fiery azures of a tropic sky and sea. Oppressive as nightmare, a formless, nameless fatigue, heavier than any burden the slaves of the mines must bear, lies forever at his heart: All deliriums of love and wine, the agonizing ecstasy of drugs, even the deepest and the faintest pulse of delight or pain—all are proven, all are futile, for the outworn but insatiate emperor. Even for a new grief, or a subtler pang than any felt before, he thinks, lying on his bed of ebony, that he would give the silver and vermilion of all his mines, with the crowded caskets, the carcanets and crowns that lie in his most immemorial treasure-vault. Vainly, with the verse of the most inventive poets, the fanciful purple-threaded fabrics of the subtlest looms, the unfamiliar gems and minerals from the uttermost land, the pallid leaves and blood-like petals of a rare and venomous blossom—vainly, with all these, and many stranger devices, wilder, more wonderful diversions, the slaves and sultanas have sought to alleviate the iron hours. One by one he has dismissed them with a weary gesture. And now, in the silence of the heavily curtained alcove, he lies alone, with the canker of ennui at his heart, like the undying mordant worm at the heart of the dead.

Anon, from between the curtains at the head of his couch, a dark and slender hand is slowly extended, clasping a dagger whose blade reflects the gold of the curtain in a thin and stealthily wavering gleam: Slowly, in silence, the dagger is poised, then rises and falls like a splinter of lightning. The emperor cries out, as the blade, piercing his loosely folded robe, wounds him slightly in the side. In a moment the alcove is filled with armed attendants, who seize and drag forth the would-be assassin—a slave girl, the princess of a conquered people, who has often, but vainly, implored her freedom from the emperor. Pale and panting with terror and rage, she faces Chan and the guardsmen, while stories of unimaginable monstrous tortures, of dooms unnameable, crowd upon her memory. But Chan, aroused and startled only for the instant, feels again the insuperable weariness, more strong than anger or fear, and delays to give the expected signal. And then, momentarily moved, perchance, by some ironical emotion, half-akin to gratitude—gratitude for the brief but diverting danger, which has served to alleviate his ennui for a little, he bids them free the princess; and, with a regal courtesy, places about her throat his own necklace of pearls and emeralds, each of which is the cost of an army.

The Memnons of the Night

Ringed with a bronze horizon, which, at a point immensely remote, seems welded with the blue brilliance of a sky of steel, they oppose the black splendour of their porphyritic forms to the sun's insuperable gaze. Reared in the morning twilight of primeval time, by a race whose towering tombs and cities are one with the dust of their builders in the slow lapse of the desert, they abide to face the terrible latter dawns, that move abroad in a starkness of fire, consuming the veils of night on the vast and Sphinx-like desolations. Level with the light, their tenebrific brows preserve a pride as of Titan kings. In their lidless implacable eyes of staring stone, is the petrified despair of those who have gazed too long on the infinite.

Mute as the mountains from whose iron matrix they were hewn, their mouths have never acknowledged the sovereignty of the suns, that pass in triumphal flame from horizon unto horizon of the prostrate land. Only at eve, when the west is like a brazen furnace, and the far-off mountains smoulder like ruddy gold in the depth of the heated heavens— only at eve, when the east grows infinite and vague, and the shadows of the waste are one with the increasing shadow of night—then, and then only, from the sullen throats of stone, a music rings to the bronze horizon—a strong, a sombre music, strange and sonorous, like the singing of black stars, or a litany of gods that invoke oblivion; a music that thrills the desert to its heart of adamant, and trembles in the granite of forgotten tombs, till the last echoes of its jubilation, terrible as the trumpets of doom, are one with the black silence of infinity.

The Garden and the Tomb

I know a garden of flowers—flowers lovely and multiform as the orchids of far, exotic worlds—as the flowers of manifold petal, whose colours change as if by enchantment in the alter nation of the triple suns; flowers like tiger lilies from the garden of Satan; like the paler lilies of paradise, or the amaranths on whose perfect and immortal beauty the seraphim so often ponder; flowers fierce and splendid like the crimson or golden flowers of fire; flowers bright and cold as the crystal flowers of snow; flowers whereof there is no likeness in any world of any sun; which have no symbol in heaven or in hell.

Alas! in the heart of the garden is a tomb—a tomb so trellised and embowered with vine and blossom, that the sunlight reveals the ghastly gleam of its marble to no careless or incurious scrutiny. But in the night, when all the flowers are still, and their perfumes are faint as the breathing of children in slumber— then, and then only, the serpents bred of corruption crawl from the tomb, and trail the fetor and phosphorescence of their abiding-place from end to end of the garden.

In Cocaigne

It was a windless afternoon of April, beneath skies that were tender as the smile of love, when we went forth, you and I, to seek the fabulous and fortunate realm of Cocaigne. Past leafing oaks with foliage of bronze and chrysolite, through zones of yellow and white and red and purple flowers, like a landscape seen through a prism, we fared with hopeful and tremulous hearts, forgetting all save the dream we had cherished. At last we came to the lonely woods, the pines with their depth of balmy, cool, compassionate shadow, which are sacred to the genius of that land. There, for the first time I was bold to take your hand in mine, and led you to a slope where the woodland lilies, with petals of white and yellow ivory, gleamed among the fallen needles. As in a dream, I found that my arms were about you, as in a dream I kissed your yielding lips, and the ardent pallor of your cheeks and throat. Motionless, you clung to me, and a flush arose beneath my kisses like a delicate stain, and lingered softly. Your eyes deepened to my gaze like the brown pools of the forest at evening, and far within them, as in immensity itself, trembled and shone the steadfast stars of your love. As a ship that has wandered beneath stormy suns and disastrous moons, but comes at last to the arms of the shielding harbour, my head lay on the gentle heaving of your delicious breast, and I knew that we had found Cocaigne.

The Litany of the Seven Kisses

I

I kiss thy hands—thy hands, whose fingers are delicate and pale as the petals of the white lotus.

II

I kiss thy hair, which has the lustre of black jewels, and is darker than Lethe, flowing by midnight through the moonless slumber of poppy-scented lands.

III

I kiss thy brow, which resembles the rising moon in a valley of cedars.

IV

I kiss thy cheeks, where lingers a faint flush, like the reflection of a rose upheld to an urn of alabaster.

V

I kiss thine eyelids, and liken them to the purple-veinèd flowers that close beneath the oppression of a tropic evening, in a land where the sunsets are bright as the flames of burning amber.

VI

I kiss thy throat, whose ardent pallor is the pallor of marble warmed by the autumn sun.

VII

I kiss thy mouth, which has the savour and perfume of fruits agleam with spray from a magic fountain, in the secret Paradise that we alone shall find; a Paradise whence they that come shall nevermore depart, for the waters thereof are Lethe, and the fruit is the fruit of the tree of Life.

From a Letter

Will you not join me in Atlantis, where we will go down through streets of blue and yellow marble to the wharves of orichalch, and choose us a galley with a golden Eros for figurehead, and sails of Tyrian sendal? With mariners that knew Odysseus, and beautiful amber-breasted slaves from the mountain-vales of Lemuria, we will lift anchor for the unknown fortunate isles of the outer sea; and, sailing in the wake of an opal sunset, will lose that ancient land in the glaucous twilight, and see from our couch of ivory and satin the rising of unknown stars and perished planets. Perhaps we will not return, but will follow the tropic summer from isle to halcyon isle, across the amaranthine seas of myth and fable: We will eat the lotos, and the fruit of lands whereof Odysseus never dreamt; and drink the pallid wines of faery, grown in a vale of perpetual moonlight. I will find for you a necklace of rosy-tinted pearls, and a necklace of yellow rubies, and crown you with precious corals that have the semblance of sanguine-coloured blossoms. We will roam in the marts of forgotten cities of jasper, and carnelian-builded ports beyond Cathay; and I will buy you a gown of peacock azure damascened with copper and gold and vermilion; and a gown of black samite with runes of orange, woven by fantastic sorcery without the touch of hands, in a dim land of spells and philtres.

From the Crypts of Memory

Aeons of aeons ago, in an epoch whose marvelous worlds have crumbled, and whose mighty suns are less than shadow, I dwelt in a star whose course, decadent from the high, irremeable heavens of the past, was even then verging upon the abyss in which, said astronomers, its immemorial cycle should find a dark and disastrous close.

Ah, strange was that gulf-forgotten star—how stranger than any dream of dreamers in the spheres of to-day, or than any vision that hath soared upon visionaries, in their retrospection of the sidereal past! There, through cycles of a history whose piled and bronze-writ records were hopeless of tabulation, the dead had come to outnumber infinitely the living. And built of a stone that was indestructible save in the furnace of suns, their cities rose beside those of the living like the prodigious metropli of Titans, with walls that overgloom the vicinal villages. And over all was the black funereal vault of the cryptic heavens—a dome of infinite shadows, where the dismal sun, suspended like a sole, enormous lamp, failed to illumine, and drawing back its fires from the face of the irresolvable ether, threw a baffled and despairing beam on the vague remote horizons, and shrouded vistas illimitable of the visionary land.

We were a sombre, secret, many-sorrowed people—we who dwelt beneath that sky of eternal twilight, pierced by the towering tombs and obelisks of the past. In our blood was the chill of the ancient night of time; and our pulses flagged with a creeping prescience of the lentor of Lethe. Over our courts and fields, like invisible sluggish vampires born of mausoleums, rose and hovered the black hours, with wings that distilled a malefic languor made from the shadowy woe and despair of perished cycles. The very skies were fraught with oppression, and we breathed beneath them as in a sepulcher, forever sealed with all its stagnancies of corruption and slow decay, and darkness impenetrable save to the fretting worm.

Vaguely we lived, and loved as in dreams—the dim and mystic dreams that hover upon the verge of fathomless sleep. We felt for our women, with their pale and spectral beauty, the same desire that the dead may feel for the phantom lilies of Hadean meads. Our days were spent in roaming through the ruins of lone and immemorial cities, whose palaces of fretted copper, and streets that ran between lines of carven golden obelisks, lay dim and ghastly with the dead light, or were drowned forever in seas of stagnant shadow; cities whose vast and iron-builded fanes preserved their gloom of primordial mystery and awe, from which the simulacra of century-forgotten gods looked forth with unalterable eyes to the hopeless heavens, and saw the ulterior night, the ultimate oblivion. Languidly we kept our gardens, whose grey lilies concealed a necromantic perfume, that had power to evoke for us the dead and spectral dreams of the past. Or, wandering through ashen fields of perennial autumn, we sought the rare and mystic immorteles, with sombre leaves and pallid petals, that bloomed beneath willows of wan and veil like foliage: or wept with a sweet and nepenthe-laden dew by the flowing silence of Acherontic waters.

And one by one we died and were lost in the dust of accumulated time. We knew the years as a passing of shadows, and death itself as the yielding of twilight unto night.

A Phantasy

I have dreamt of an unknown land—a land remote in ulterior time, and alien space not ascertainable: the desert of a long-completed past, upon which has settled the bleak, irrevocable silence of infinitude; where all is ruined save the stone of tombs and cenotaphs; and where the sole peoples are the kingless, uncounted tribes of the subterranean dead.

Above this land of my dream, citied with tombs and cenotaphs, a red and smouldering sun maintains a spectral day, in alternation with an ashen moon through the black ether where the stars have long since perished. And through the hush of the consummation of time, above the riven monuments and crumbled records of alien history, flit in the final twilight the mysterious wings of seraphim, sent to fulfill ineffable errands, or confer with demons of the abyss; and black, gigantic angels, newly returned from missions of destruction, pause amid the sepulchers to sift from their gloomy and tremendous vans the pale ashes of annihilated stars.

The Demon, The Angel, And Beauty

Of the Demon who standeth or walketh always with me at my left hand, I asked: "Hast thou seen Beauty? Her that me-seemeth was the mistress of my soul in Eternity? Her that is now beyond question set over me in Time; even though I behold her not, and, it may be, have never beheld, nor ever shall; her of whose aspect I am ignorant as noon is concerning any star; her of whom as witness and testimony, I have found only the hem of her shadow, or at most, her reflection in a dim and troubled water. Answer, if thou canst, and tell me, is she like pearls, or like stars? Does she resemble most the sunlight that is transparent and unbroken, or the sunlight divided into splendour and iris? Is she the heart of the day, or the soul of the night?"

To which the Demon answered, after, as I thought, a brief space of meditation:

"Concerning this Beauty, I can tell thee but little beyond that which thou knowest. Albeit, in those orbs to which the demons of my rank have admission, there be greater adumbrations of some transcendent Mystery than here, yet have I never seen that Mystery itself, and know not if it be male or female. Aeons ago, when I was young and incautious, when the world was new and bright, and there were more stars than now,

I, too was attracted by this Mystery, and sought after it in all accessible spheres. But failing to find the thing itself, I soon grew weary of embracing its shadows, and took to the pursuit of illusions less insubstantial. Now I am become grey and ashen without, and red like old fire within, who was fiery and flame-coloured all through, back in the star-thronged aeons of which I speak: Heed me, for I am as wise, and wary and ancient as the far-travelled and comet-scarred sun; and I am become of the opinion that the thing Beauty itself does not exist. Doubtless the semblance thereof is but a web of shadow and delusion, woven by the crafty hand of God, that He may snare demons and men therewith, for His mirth, and the laughter of His archangels."

The Demon ceased, and took to watching me as usual—obliquely, and with one eye—an eye that is more red than Aldebaran, and inscrutable as the gulfs beyond the Hyades.

Then of the Angel, who walketh or standeth always with me at my right hand, I asked, "Hast thou seen Beauty? Or hast thou heard any assured rumour concerning Beauty?"

To which the Angel answered, after, as I thought, a moment of hesitation:

"As to this Beauty, I can tell thee but little beyond that which thou knowest. Albeit in all the heavens, this

Mystery is a topic of the most frequent and sublime speculation among the archangels, and a perennial theme for the more inspired singers and harpists of the cherubim—yea, despite all this, we are greatly ignorant as to its true nature, and substance, and attributes. But sometimes there are mighty adumbrations which cover even the superior seraphim from above their wing-tips, and make unfamiliar twilight in heaven. And sometimes there is an echo which fills the empyrean, and hushes the archangelic harps in the midst of their praising of God. This is not often, and these visitations of echo and shadow spread an awe over the assembled Thrones and Splendours and Dominations, which at other times accompanies only the emanence or appearance of God Himself. Thus are we assured as to the reality of this Beauty. And because it remains a mystery to us, to whom naught else is mysterious except God, we conjecture that it is the thing upon which God meditateth, self-obscured and centred, and because of which He hath held himself immanifest to us for so many aeons; that this is the secret which God keepeth even from the seraphim."

The Shadows

There were many shadows in the palace of Augusthes. About the silver throne that had blackened beneath the invisible passing of ages, they fell from pillar and broken roof and fretted window in ever-shifting multiformity. Seeming the black, fantastic spectres of doom and desolation, they moved through the palace in a gradual, grave, and imperceptible dance, whose music was the change and motion of suns and moons. They were long and slender, like all other shadows before the early light, and behind the declining sun; squat and intense beneath the desert noontide, and faint with the withered moon; and in the interlunar darkness, they were as myriad tongues hidden behind the shut and silent lips of night.

One came daily to that place of shadows and desolation, and sate upon the silver throne, watching the shadows that were of desolation. King nor slave disputed him there, in the palace whose kings and whose slaves were powerless alike in the intangible dungeon of centuries. The tombs of unnumbered and forgotten monarchs were white upon the yellow desert roundabout. Some had partly rotted away, and showed like the sunken eye-sockets of a skull—blank and lidless beneath the staring heavens; others still retained the undesecrated seal of death, and were as the closed eyes of one lately dead. But he who watched the shadows from the silver throne, heeded not these, nor the fleet wind that dipt to the broken tombs, and emerged shrilly, its unseen hands dark with the dust of kings.

He was a philosopher, from what land there was none to know or ask. Nor was there any to ask what knowledge or delight he sought in the ruined palace, with eyes alway upon the moving shadows; nor what were the thoughts that moved through his mind in ghostly unison with them. His eyes were old and sad with meditation and wisdom; and his beard was long and white upon his long white robe.

For many days he came with the dawn and departed with sunset; and his shadow leaned from the shadow of the throne and moved with the others. But one eve he departed not; and thereafter his shadow was one with the shadow of the silver throne. Death found and left him there, where he dwindled into dust that was as the dust of slaves or kings.

But the ebb and refluence of shadows went on, in the days that were before the end; ere the aged world, astray with the sun in strange heavens, should be lost in the cosmic darkness, or, under the influence of other and conflicting gravitations, should crumble apart and bare its granite bones to the light of strange suns, and the granite, too, should dissolve, and be as of the dust of slaves and kings. Noon was encircled with darkness, and the depths of palace-dusk were chasmed with sunlight. Change there was none, other than this, for the earth was dead, and stirred not to the tottering feet of time. And in the expectant silence before the twilight of the sun, the moving shadows seemed but a mockery of change; a meaningless antic phantasmagoria of things that were; an afterfiguring of forgotten time.

And now the sun was darkened slowly in mid-heaven, as by some vast and invisible bulk. And twilight hushed the shadows in the palace of Augusthes, as the world itself swung down toward the long and single shadow of irretrievable oblivion.

Safe Space

In my room, moths assail me.
The parks are thick with mosquitoes,
and the mating birds swoop the fields.

The light blinds, and the dark deafens.

The cold controls body and the heat distorts mind.

Give me sunrise at midday,

quiet noise, and

life from a distance.

Give me limitless space that I may fill,

whilst I inflate as an infinite mote of dust.

- Jonathon Best
16th October, 2022

ISBN: 978-0-9953520-2-5